A WAY BACK TO THEN

ROBERT HALLIWELL

Published by
DREAMSPINNER PRESS

5032 Capital Circle SW, Suite 2, PMB# 279, Tallahassee, FL 32305-7886 USA
http://www.dreamspinnerpress.com/

This is a work of fiction. Names, characters, places, and incidents either are the product of author imagination or are used fictitiously, and any resemblance to actual persons, living or dead, business establishments, events, or locales is entirely coincidental.

A Way Back to Then
© 2015 Robert Halliwell.

Cover Art
© 2015 Paul Richmond.
http://www.paulrichmondstudio.com
Cover content is for illustrative purposes only and any person depicted on the cover is a model.

ISBN: 978-1-63216-959-4
Digital ISBN: 978-1-63216-960-0
Library of Congress Control Number: 2015902237
First Edition June 2015

Printed in the United States of America
∞
This paper meets the requirements of
ANSI/NISO Z39.48-1992 (Permanence of Paper).

For all of us who believe in the magic within ourselves.

Acknowledgments

I'm not good at this kind of thing, but I suppose I should thank John Goode first since he was the one who had faith in me and kicked me in the ass to write this book. Plus, if I don't say something, I'll never hear the end of it and/or he might kill me off in his next book.

However, one person that both of us can agree needs special recognition is Gayle. Without her we both would be lost and missing a voice of reasoning and especially grammar.

Thank you to my family and friends for the outpouring of support, especially my husband, Kevin, who continues to let me have mini-meltdowns at least twice a day and sticks around regardless.

I also want to take a minute to acknowledge those people whom I might not get to express my deepest gratitude to in real life because they're fancy and I would most likely pass out if I ever met them. Elizabeth, Anne, and the entire staff at Dreamspinner for taking a chance on me. Jeff Bowen and Hunter Bell for helping me believe dreams are real. Bobby Lopez and Kristen Anderson-Lopez for an anthem that has saved me from me. Alan Menken and Howard Ashman for writing the soundtrack of my childhood and most of my adulthood.

And finally, Mr. Stephen Sondheim for being my personal lord and savior.

Preface

I ADJUSTED the rearview mirror and saw the reflection of a blond-haired boy wearing a graduation gown grow smaller as I drove out of the high school parking lot. When I knew I was a safe distance away, I pulled the car to the side of the deserted road and cried for what seemed like hours. Luckily, most of the town was at Foster High, so there was very little chance that someone would spot a grown-ass man bawling his eyes out in a lime-green VW Bug.

I opened the glove compartment for some tissue and a stack of napkins from the Bear's Den fell out. I watched them fall to the car floor. Each represented a memory I had of that place. Good, bad, and horrific. I met some of my best friends at that little hole in the middle of nothing where I could be the real me without any judgment.

It was also the place where I experienced the worst moment of my life.

I stuffed the napkins back into the glove compartment, not wanting to lose the memories or even the smell of the Bear's Den. I wiped my face and nose, thinking not about the one bad night that happened a lifetime ago, but instead about last night when I went there for a mini-bon-voyage party that my friends Tom, Tyler, and Tyler's boyfriend, Matt, were throwing for me.

"TO ROBBIE," Tom said as we all raised our glasses, "one of the biggest bitches and best friends a man could ever want."

I was about to protest the bitch part, but the tearful wink Tom gave me told me he was joking and serious at the same time.

We each took a sip of what passes for champagne in this godforsaken part of town. Tyler downed his glass in one gulp.

"Slow down there, babe," Matt said to his boyfriend. "I don't want to have to roll you out of here tonight."

Tyler smiled slightly and looked at me before quickly turning back to Matt.

"So." Tom cleared his throat. "What time are you leaving so the munchkin parade can start?"

I flipped him off, and he laughed.

"The moving company is coming to pick up my car late tomorrow afternoon to be shipped up to New York, and my flight is the following morning." I looked over at a rather uncomfortable and slightly intoxicated Tyler. "I'm going to have to cut out before the end of graduation."

Tyler looked like I just kicked him right square in the balls.

"You can't do that to the kids!" He tried to get up but slumped back down with Matt's help.

"They'll live, Tyler," I said calmly. "They're young and will get over it quickly."

"But...," Tyler said as the tears started to flow. "But what about the kids?"

Matt looked at his boyfriend like he was a five-year-old complaining about the socks he got for Christmas, while Tom was wiping his own wet face. We all knew this wasn't about the kids; this was about me and him.

I sighed and walked over to Tyler, who was at my eye level since he was sitting, and I wrapped my arms around him. I saw Matt tense up out of the corner of my eye as Tyler buried his head into my shoulder and cried. I didn't say anything. I held him tight and rubbed his back until he calmed down a bit and stopped using my shirt as a snot rag. I tried not to look at the pair of eyes that were staring at me from the bulletin board in front of me.

I failed.

Tyler raised his head a little and rested his chin on my shoulder. "You promise you're going to call me? Or Spyke me when you're up there?"

I laughed and pulled away from Tyler, making sure I gave Matt an *At ease, soldier* glance. "Yes, Tyler, I will call or Skype you when I'm back and settled. And you can do the same when you get sick of constantly talking to this moose over here." I smirked at Matt, and he laughed nervously. I think we were still on the fence on whether or not we liked each other.

Tyler smiled. At my little jest or because he was head over ass in love with the moose, I would never know.

"All right. Enough of this fairy shit," Tom bellowed. "Another round, and no more goddamn crying."

Thank God Tom wasn't here to see me now.

I shoved the tissues back into the glove compartment and shut the door.

I looked at the time and saw that the car movers would be at my house within the hour. I pulled myself together as best as possible and drove the couple of blocks to my old store. I still hadn't given back the keys to the landlord and most likely never would.

I parked my car in my usual spot for the last time and got out. I unlocked the door to my second home for the past two years and slowly opened it.

The place was dark and empty except for a few racks and hangers scattered on the floor. I closed my eyes and took a deep breath. Memories flowed in my head of Foster people coming in here, not knowing what the hell just sprang up in the middle of town, with a colorful homo standing behind the store counter giving them all a welcoming but evil look.

The act I put on became a lifestyle. I packed the old, real me into a small cage inside my bitter and angry heart. It wasn't until a floppy-haired and terrified teenager with worn-out clothes came through that very same door that the bars of my cage started to melt.

After that, everything in my life had been a butterfly effect—right up to now.

I opened my eyes and knew I had one last thing to do before I closed this part of my life for good.

I found an old sign, flipped it over to the blank white side, and placed it on the counter. I went to the storeroom and found a red Magic Marker and brought it back to my makeshift canvas.

I carefully wrote the words out in big, bold print and colored in the letters. Satisfied, I gave my creation a nod of approval and hung it in the window. I wasn't sure how long it was going be up there, but I hoped the people it was meant for would see it before someone took it down. I took one last look around and, before I started to lose it again, I walked out of the empty shell of a store and locked the door behind me.

I started my car and looked at the sign I had hung in the window.

"Make your own happy ending," I read out loud.

I smiled proudly.

"You're damn right I will."

Chapter One
Clicking Your Heels You Don't Get Too Far

I FOLLOWED the line of people to the baggage claim in Long Island's small, but convenient, MacArthur Airport and turned my cell phone on. As it tried to grab some sort of signal, the voice mail alert chimed three times, indicating I had that same number of messages.

All of them from my mother, naturally.

The first was a hang-up.

The second was sort of a message. "Hello? Robert? You there? Did the plane land yet? Hello?" and then it cut off.

The last was her simply saying, "I'm out front," but was almost a minute long because she didn't hit the End button correctly. I had to listen to her rendition of "Poker Face" for fifty-eight seconds.

I think I'll save that message for special occasions.

My mother still has no idea how to use the iPhone I bought her last Christmas. Just in case you were wondering.

My three pieces of luggage came around the winding treadmill thing, and I plucked them off quickly before they got too far. I made my way to the automatic door, and there was my mother sitting in her silver Mercedes, playing what I could only assume was Angry Birds on her phone, because it was the only thing she knew how to do with her phone.

I rolled my suitcases over to the car and tapped on the passenger window. She jumped in her seat and gaped at me with a face of terror. When she realized it was me and not some carjacker, she smiled brightly. She flung open the door and didn't bother to shut it before rushing over to me with her arms wide open.

"My baby boy has come home!" she squealed as she cut off the flow of oxygen into my lungs by bear-hugging me. "I've missed you so much!" She kissed each of my cheeks roughly seventy-two times.

"Ma," I choked in between the assaults, "I just saw you at Christmas, and we Skyped every week."

"Yes," she said and finally released me. "But this time you're home for good." She gave me another hug, this time not as violent.

I was about to respond with "Temporarily" when the car behind my mother's honked at us.

If you had told me I was going back to living with my mother years after I turned thirty, I would have laughed at you while jumping up and down on your chest for even suggesting such a thing. Lo and behold, there I was in her car, returning to the place I'd wanted to leave so desperately almost ten years ago.

It wasn't that I hated living with my family. Far from it, in fact. They were the only ones who kept me sane all those times I thought about hitchhiking to Canada and never looking back. Going from a comfortable two-bedroom house back to a twelve-by-twelve bedroom where I'd had wet dreams about Patrick Swayze wasn't exactly on my list of life goals.

"Hey, asshole!" my mother screamed. "You can't wait one more goddamn minute for me to welcome my son back home?" And she flipped the driver off.

You've got to love my warm yet crazy, loud, Sicilian through and through mother. You may risk taking the girl out of Brooklyn, but try as you might, you'll never take Brooklyn out of the girl.

She turned back to me, smiled, and gave my right cheek a squeeze. "*Face bello!*" she said, pronouncing it fah-chay, and hit the button on her car remote to open the trunk. I loaded up my luggage and got into the passenger seat, making sure my seat belt was taut. I love my mother, but she can't drive for shit.

"Did my car get delivered all right?" I asked as she peeled out of the airport parking lot, making me grab the *oh fuck!* handle above me. Thank God the house was only two miles away.

"Yes," she said. "It came early this afternoon. Honey, don't be upset, but I think they scratched it while it was coming up here from Texas."

"Christ. Where?" I asked, annoyed already. That car was the only thing that had survived Foster along with me. I know I hadn't taken perfect care of her, but the thought of something happening to Elphaba—because what else do you name a lime-green Bug?—chilled me to the bone.

"The driver's side," she said.

I let out the breath I'd been holding. "Under the mirror?"

"Yes. How did you know that?" she asked.

"Ma," I said as I face-palmed, "I did that two years ago with a shopping cart. Remember? I told you about that."

"Oh." She slumped. "Oh! That's right! I completely forgot. Well, you got $500 back on your credit card regardless because I ripped that bastard moving company a new one over the phone, so you're welcome." She turned and beamed smugly at me.

"Ma! The road!" I yelled as we started to veer off to the left.

"Shit. Sorry," she said, readjusting her focus.

I looked at her and shook my head, then laughed. My mother is one of those people who still believes we live in an age where the customer is always right, even if they're 110 percent wrong. For example, she once had a very expensive alarm system put in the house totally free of charge because she thought the salesman was first, checking out her ass, and second, overcharging her. She ended up calling the guy's manager, and then called that guy's manager just in case, to let them know she would go to News 12 with the story.

Needless to say, no one knows if the guy checked out my mom's ass—gross—or if she was overcharged or if the alarm company really thought she had a friend at the local cable station. I personally think they didn't want to hear her bitch any longer.

Over the past twenty-something years, my mom has become, you might say, hostile toward many things that disrupt her life. If I had a degree in psychology, I would be comfortable saying that the hostility dates to certain events that changed her both emotionally and mentally.

My father died when I was only five and my mother was still pregnant with my sister, Nicole. He was sideswiped by a drunk driver late one night while he was coming home from work. The guy hit my father's car hard enough to make it flip over on the Southern State Parkway. My father died instantly. The drunk was also killed because he hit a tree and wasn't wearing a seat belt.

My father's life insurance took care of most of the bills for a while. Unfortunately it wasn't long until my mother had to go back to work at the local bank, where she ended up meeting her second husband.

He was a well-off bank manager whose wife had passed not too long before my father. After almost eight years of his pursuit of my mother, they started dating and eventually got married. She quit her job at the bank because she didn't feel right working for her husband and it wasn't financially necessary for her to work. He was nice enough to me and my sister the short time they were married, but even at my young age, there was something I didn't trust about him. When I was in my junior year of high school, my mother started to have suspicions and not trust him either. She found out, through various sources, that he had been sleeping with his young assistant since about three months into his marriage with my mother.

It's a story my mother loves to hate to tell.

You would think my mother would have gone all Angela Bassett in *Waiting to Exhale* on him, but instead she calmly went to another branch of the bank in the next town over and completely drained their joint accounts dry. She explained what her husband had done, and the tellers were happy to oblige. Some even said that they knew he was hooking up with the girl but were afraid to lose their jobs if they told. My mother thanked them, deposited the money in a different bank, and went back to the house to wait until he got home that night.

When he arrived he screamed at my mother about the money while she just sat at the table drinking her afternoon tea. Before he had a heart attack from all the stress, he stopped screaming and she finally spoke.

"I know about her" was all she said.

The color drained from his face, but he tried to deny it. When my mother said she had witnesses, he looked like he was about to drop dead right then and there.

He moved out that night to who knows where, and from what my mother told me, she never saw him again. Not even in the divorce hearings where she got everything she wanted and more.

Cut to my mother having the house completely redone, a new car, a built-in pool with its very own fully functional pool house, and Nicole and I having our tuition paid in full.

"My first husband and soul mate was killed," she would say, "and my second husband was a cheating son of a bitch. If I didn't gag at the thought of having sex with a woman, I would've become a lesbian years ago." She hadn't remarried or even dated anyone since.

We pulled into the driveway, and I saw my car sitting there, shining like it was new.

"I cleaned it up and tried to get as much of Texas out of it as I could," my mother said as she turned off her car.

"Thanks, Ma. You didn't have to do that," I said to her.

"I know I didn't, but I'm your mother, so shut up." And she winked at me.

We got out of the car and took out my luggage. She grabbed the smaller suitcase while I tried to roll the other two over the stone driveway.

"All your boxes came earlier this week," she told me as she unlocked the front door. "I had the movers put them back in the pool house for you to go through. I would've done some laundry, but I couldn't figure out what box was what."

"It's all right," I said. "I'll get to it eventually."

"Why don't you go back there and organize some of that crap while I start dinner?" she said with a weird tone.

"Ma, I just want to go upstairs and relax right now," I whined. "I'm exhausted."

She gave me a look. It was the same look she'd had when she knew I got into her makeup when I was eight. "Robert Joseph DeCaro, I said go back there and start unpacking," she snarled through her clenched teeth, which only a mother can do, and tossed me the keys to unlock the pool house door.

"Yes, Mommie Dearest," I responded and scurried straight out the back door before she had a chance to throw her shoe at me. I walked around the pool to the minihouse in back.

Bracing myself for the smell of chlorine-drenched inflatable toys and recently cleaned beach towels, I unlocked the door. Instead there was a pleasant fragrance of vanilla. It was dark inside, so I felt the wall for the light switch and flipped it on.

My jaw went slack at what I saw in front of me.

If I said she went all out, that would be an understatement. My mother had converted the once underused pool house into a real home. It looked like a one-bedroom apartment on steroids. The walls were painted in earth tones and covered in various Broadway show posters I thought my mother had thrown out years ago. She must have reframed them all because they looked brand new, not covered in cobwebs like the last time I saw them. There was a small kitchen complete with mini-appliances that led to a full-size bathroom with a shower and tub.

The living/dining area had a brand-new couch, love seat, and table. My big-screen television fit in the corner as well as the rack for my 500 DVDs. I had sold most of my furniture before I left, so it was nice to have new things. I walked over to a door to my left and opened it. It was my new bedroom. Two new dressers, a walk-in closet, and a queen-size four-poster bed complete with nightstands filled the space perfectly.

A weak smile appeared on my face and tears filled my eyes as I looked at the bed. The mattress and bed set I had in Foster were the last things I threw out before I left. The bed was the first thing Riley and I had bought together when we moved into the house. No one had and no one would ever sleep in that bed except us.

The bed in front of me would be only mine.

I looked over to the nightstand to the right and focused on the picture frame that stood on it.

If my eyes were misty before, they were a tidal wave now.

The picture was a five-by-seven photo of Riley and me with our arms around each other in front of the packed taxi that was taking us to the airport. My mom had taken the picture just as we were about to leave for our new life in Texas. It had taken her ten shots to get a halfway decent one because she was crying and shaking the whole time.

She'd loved Riley like he was one of her own. Nicole had loved him like a second brother, and I had often wondered if they liked him better than they liked me. I picked up the frame and touched the glass.

"So," my mother's voice came from behind me, "what do you think?"

I put the frame back on the small table and turned around just in time to see her face darken for a split second when she looked at the picture. She quickly smiled before making eye contact with me.

I walked over to her and pulled her into a hug. "It's perfect, Ma. Thank you."

She squeezed back. "Anything for you, my little bubbie." She pulled away from me. "You sure everything is good?"

"Yes, Ma. I love it all," I said with a smile. I squinted my eyes and continued speculatively. "Something tells me you had some help with all this, though." I did my best Vanna White impression, including the entire apartment in one sweep of my hand.

"Uh... well?" she stammered. "I did have some help."

I love my mother, but her interior design skills are a bit on the scary side. She goes through phases. When we were younger, every room except for the bedrooms had something to do with dogs. Don't even ask about the schnauzer toilet seat cover.

When Riley and I first started dating, she had the idea of theming everything in Western motif. Cowboy hats and horses galore! I tried to explain that even real Texans don't have that shit on every surface they own.

"Let me guess," I said, knowing exactly who had amazing decorating skills. "Uncle James?"

"Good guess," she answered, smiling at her only brother's name.

"How is the old queen these days?" I asked.

Uncle James and my mother were as tight as Nicole and I were. They were there for each other through the best parts of their lives and the darkest. They would laugh and argue but never stayed mad with one another for more than a day. James constantly took my mom to the city to see one Broadway show after another and then have a night on the town. When Nicole and I were old enough, he piled us onto the Long Island Railroad and made sure we had the best seats in the house for the latest Broadway show he was obsessed with at least four times a year.

He was the first person I came out to because I didn't know how my mother would react. Having your brother be gay is one thing, but your son is something quite different. Uncle James told me to be honest with her and let her know how much she meant to me.

I did exactly that. When I told her, she was upset. But not for the reason I thought. She was pissed that I'd come out to him before her. Not because she thought I was too scared to tell her, but because they had a bet on who I was going to show my rainbow flag to first.

"Mothers always know" is the expression, isn't it?

As you can tell by now, my mother couldn't care less who I slept with as long as they treated me with love and respect.

My mother's face lost a little light when I asked about my uncle. "He's... coping," she said quietly. "I think maybe you should go visit him when you get the chance."

"I should've been here for him" was all I could say.

"Robert," she said sternly. "You had plenty of things to deal with down there. James knows how much you care for him, and he understands that you couldn't get away from that godforsaken town without hitching up a horse and buggy to drive to the nearest airport." She paused. "You're home now, and that's all that matters."

"I'll stop by there tomorrow," I said.

"Good," she said. "Now get yourself ready for dinner. It's almost done." She stood on her toes, kissed my cheek, and then lightly smacked it. "And pick up all this shit." She motioned to my bags and walked out the door.

And just like that, I was home.

When I was younger, I didn't have many friends. Our neighbors were mostly older with kids who were already in college by the time I started first grade. In school I was quiet and stuck to myself. No one bothered me and I never bothered them. That lasted all the way through high school, where there were so many kids that, unless you drove up in a new Mercedes, no one noticed you. With the money my mother received from my dad's life insurance and her eventual divorce settlement, she was able to send my sister and me to a "decent" school as opposed to the public school we lived near.

It was a Catholic school. Everybody wore the same uniform, and I was able to camouflage myself with the rest of the crowd. I remember at graduation, when they called my name to receive my diploma, I only heard the sound of cheers coming from my mother, sister, my uncles James and Andy—yeah, they're a couple; I'll get to that part in a bit—and the quiet clapping of the strange girl I had a semifriendship with in art club. Maybe the applause would've been louder if the club had more than two members.

Let me just say here that I wasn't a depressed, lonely child who was scared of losing someone like I had when my father died.

That came later in life.

When the accident happened, my mother explained that my father had gone to live with the angels but would always be with us. I, like most five-year-olds who had just lost a parent, looked at her and said, "Okay," gave her a hug, and went back to watching *Sesame Street*. I didn't understand death back then; looking back I realize it was because I hadn't really met her yet.

The whole time Nic and I were growing up, my uncle, who essentially became our own fairy godfather, would take my sister and me to the movies to see the latest Disney features. Sometimes we went to the ancient theater in town where they would show classic films, animated and live action, on the big screen for a dollar. I would watch in amazement at the beauty of animation and music coming together on-screen. Being the curious kid I was, I noticed that most of the time, I was drawn to the main character having only one living parent. Somehow it made me feel better that the pretty heroine was just like me. Whether her father or mother was or wasn't there, she still ended up doing okay in the end.

Whenever those movies finally came out on VHS, I would beg my mother to bring me to Sam Goody to buy it the day it came out. I'd even write the release date on the calendar in bright red ink. I would rip open the cellophane as soon as I got home and proceed to watch the movie on heavy rotation for the next week, singing and dancing along with my new friend on the television.

If you don't think people are born gay, I have news for you: we most certainly are. I would dream that my house was covered in thorns and my family and I were eagerly waiting for the handsome prince to come save us.

TRANSFIXED BY the visions in front of me, my brain melted the basic plot of those movies together. The main protagonist was some peculiar young girl who wanted to escape her mundane life of brushing her long hair with a kitchen utensil and cleaning up after her vile stepfamily. She dreamed of the day a prince in disguise or a bizarro weather phenomenon would literally sweep her off of her feet, taking her from the world of sepia tones to a far-off land above the ocean surface full of magical creatures basking in the warm light of Technicolor rainbows she used to read about in her favorite book.

Our heroine would then proceed to calm the beast, kill the witch, marry the wealthy prince, and dance on her own two feet with a brand-new hairstyle to boot.

And best of all, she got that coveted prize.

The happily ever after.

IT WAS something that, as I started college, I continued to daydream about, though I'd stopped binge-watching those movies years earlier. Later I realized, the hard way, that real life wasn't all castles and singing flatware.

My life ended up becoming one big fractured fairy tale. I'd just recently picked up the last piece in order to start Krazy Gluing it all back together.

Disney never makes movies about those kinds of stories.

AS AN innocent kid, I would clap at the credits and rewind the tape to relive the experience again.

As an overthinking adult, I thought, "So then what?"

Was she really going to be happy forever after? Would she ever miss her normal life? Were the worn-out clothes and animal friends she gave up secretly the things that she missed and loved the most? Didn't she get bored with just hanging around the castle under constant supervision while her husband was out fighting a giant, a dragon, or worse, his hormones? Did she look out the window at that strange vine that was reaching up into the clouds and think there was another land just waiting to be discovered?

What happened... later?

See, that's the problem with those stories. There is no later; there is just the end. You want to make a happy ending? Know when to stop your story. Life doesn't stop like that, and when it does... it isn't a happy ending at all.

AFTER A meal that could kill an elephant, I staggered back, barely missing the pool, to my new living space and dropped onto my new bed. It was so fluffy and comfortable that I passed out almost immediately. I had traveled most of the day, sure, but it was gorging on three pounds of manicotti that really did me in.

The morning sunlight stung my eyes as I slowly opened them. While they were coming into focus, I had the mini-panic attack that most of us get when we wake up in a strange environment for the first time. It took a couple of seconds for me to realize that this was my home now, far from the dry weather and Southern twangs, and instead the place of 500 percent humidity and *really* good pizza.

I walked to the front window and saw that my mother's car wasn't in the driveway. She most likely was out food shopping, since the cabinets and refrigerator must be restocked in case nuclear warfare came to Long Island. I ate some yogurt she had left in my own fridge, then took a shower and got dressed for the day.

As I made my way over to my front door to leave, I paused and turned around, taking it all in again. "This is the first day of a new life," I said to myself and then looked up to the heavens. "Please don't let me fuck it up." I waited for the music to swell and for animated bluebirds to sing me my opening song, but alas, only real birds showed up to shit on my car. I tell ya, Disney princesses do not know when they have it good. It's doubtful that pumpkin carriages are used for target practice.

I locked the door behind me, got into my car, and pulled out of the driveway, making the five-minute-long trek to my uncle's home on autopilot.

When I pulled up to the house, everything was exactly the way it had been when I left with Riley to go to Texas. The perfectly manicured lawn and the beautiful rose bushes that always bloomed this time of year looked the same as they did years back. How James kept it up alone never ceased to amaze me. As I got out of the car, I threw my cigarette into the middle of the road and popped a piece of gum in my mouth for less than thirty seconds so I wouldn't smell too smoky. I swallowed hard, regretting it instantly as the soft substance made its slow journey down my esophagus to my stomach, where it would live for the next seven years, according to Dr. Oz.

The sound of a young Barbra Streisand from the original cast recording of *Funny Girl* playing on an old Victrola flowed from the front window. I had to laugh; I didn't know how that record hadn't been scratched to hell after being played at least 5,000 times.

The music got louder as I walked up to the door and rang the bell. I took the time to really look at the house and noticed that, up close, it was not as beautiful as it had been the last time I was there. The paint around the doorframe was chipping, and the outside light was rusty and full of spiderwebs. I made a confused face because James and Andy never let anything of theirs get less than pristine.

The door unlocked and slowly opened, revealing the man who'd helped raise me to be the person I am today.

"You little shit," my uncle said.

"You old hag," I replied.

He stepped over the threshold and pulled me into a tight hug. He might be in his early sixties, but the man still had some strength in him. I wrapped my arms around him and squeezed back.

"I'm so happy you're finally home," he said quietly.

"Yeah," I said, "me too."

He pulled away but kept his hands on my shoulders. He gave me a once-over, then sniffed. "You're smoking again, aren't you?"

I rolled my eyes. "Yes, Aunt Sassy, I am."

He squinted an evil glare at the hated nickname. "You reek of it, and your breath smells like a dive bar from the eighties," he replied, disgusted.

"Thanks," I gushed, smirking. "And you look like an extra from *Leave It to Beaver*. Nice cardigan, Gramps."

He let go of my shoulders to pull at the blue sweater he was wearing. "Shut your trap," he said. "I haven't the time to do laundry, and this is one of the few clean things I own. Now get in here before the neighbors think I'm taking applications for a new pool boy."

I walked in and gasped at the state the house was in. When I was younger and came over, I had to take off my shoes at the door and make a conscious effort not to touch anything because James and Andy's home was a few velvet ropes short of a museum.

But now…. I mean, the house wasn't filthy or smelly; it was just lived-in. Some papers cluttered the dining room table; the carpets didn't have those just-vacuumed lines on them. James walked over to the record player and cut off Barbra in the middle of singing "People."

"Before you say even one cunty thing," he said, making his way back to me, "yes, I look like shit and yes, the place looks like a tornado hit it, but no, there aren't any ruby slippers hiding under the rubble, so don't go searching, Dorothy."

I just stood there and stared at him. Uncle James had always been the type of person who would put on a hazmat suit if he saw an ant crawl across the living room floor. Now, the house just looked as normal as anyone else's.

"I just haven't had the time to clean the house, my clothes, and let alone myself these past couple of years," he continued somberly.

My mother told me at dinner last night that when Andy was sick, my uncle had traveled back and forth to the hospital so much that everything, literally, had piled up all over. Uncle James looked around the mess, and his eyes started to tear up. "I just haven't had any interest in doing… anything."

Out of the corner of my eye, I saw the coatrack where I would hang my scarf and jacket whenever I came over during the winter months. The derby Andy used to wear was sitting on the top, while the cane he used when he'd hurt his knee a decade ago hung from one of the hooks. My mother told me that my uncle hadn't moved the objects since Andy suffered his fatal stroke and the ambulance took him away. He was in the hospital for four days, finally passing away a couple of days after New Year's. The hat and the cane were dust-free, as if Uncle James Swiffered them like they were just other pieces of furniture.

"How are you doing?" I swallowed hard, not wanting to know the answer.

"I have no fucking clue," he said quietly. "It's like he was here yesterday and then gone this morning."

Andy had been as healthy as a horse and I'd never thought he would die by the time he was fifty-four.

"I'm so sorry I wasn't here, Unc," I said. "Is there anything—"

He cut me off with a raised palm. "Please don't say what you're about to say, Robbie. There was nothing that you or I could've done. You were dealing with your own issues at the time, and it was over too quickly for you to get up here. Fate is a heartless bitch. I just have to make whatever time I have left on this earth worth it." He looked down at something on the ground.

Unfortunately, he was right. Andy had passed only a few months after Riley, and my mother didn't tell me until after the funeral because I was still reeling from my own loss. For a while I was upset with both of them and my sister for not letting me know, but in the end I understood why they'd done it.

Uncle James rubbed his temples when his eyes became glassy, and he wagged his finger at me. "You're not going to get me to cry, Miss Walters."

I smiled slightly. "I wouldn't dare."

My uncle and Andy were who I had wanted Riley and me to be in twenty years. They'd loved each other through some of the worst times in history to be openly gay. When James met Andy in college, they were both still dating girls, but they had instantly become inseparable and secretly dated each other behind their girlfriends' backs. They eventually broke it off with the clueless girls and moved away from city life to suburban Long Island. Their neighbors didn't think anything of the two of them being a couple because their house was constantly full of people, especially beautiful women. People thought they were just aging fraternity brothers who wanted to be forever bachelors.

Little did anyone know that James and Andy were one of the most faithful and loving couples to live on their block. Andy would come home from working at the body shop and Uncle James would chase him into the bathroom with a can of Lysol until Andy took a shower. Andy would want to watch the game while Uncle James was in the middle of his "stories" on daytime television.

Were they the perfect couple? Not at all. Is any relationship "perfect"? They had their tiffs, but that only made their relationship and love that much stronger. For every fight, there were the inevitable apologies and laughter at how stupid they'd sounded. But now there were no more pointless spats about who left the cap off the toothpaste or whose turn it was to make dinner.

I envied the both of them, even now.

"Hey, Princess." James derailed my train of thought by calling me the nickname he had used for most of my life, which I never took offense to. "Where'd you go?"

"Nowhere. Nothing," I stammered.

"Bullshit." He walked over to me. "I know that contorted face you make. You're overthinking again."

"What? No, I'm not." I tried to laugh it off.

"Now a nervous laugh?" He shook his head. "Boy, you really need to work on your lying skills." My face started to blush, a sure sign that I was caught. "What's going on with you? Talk to me."

I shook my head. "No, I can't. I'm not going to bother you with my crap. It wouldn't—"

"If you say 'it wouldn't be right,' I will crack you over the head with my Patti LuPone record collection." He must've seen the fear in my eyes, because he knew I couldn't be within twenty feet of anything related to that harpy without breaking out in hives. "Just because I've been through the gauntlet and have had two knee replacements doesn't mean I won't pick your ass up when it gets knocked down."

Whenever my mother had worked overtime, James would babysit Nicole and me. I couldn't tell you how many times I slipped and fell doing my impersonation of Olivia Newton-John in roller skates. James was there to wipe my tears, clean the boo-boos, and get me vertical again.

"Okay, okay." I held up my hands in defeat and sighed. "It's just that I wish I had more time with him."

James's shoulders dropped, and he walked slowly into the living room. "We all wish we could have more time, honey." He sat down in his fluffy chair by the fireplace and looked over at the stiffer chair across from him, the one that hadn't been occupied for a long time. "Whether it's four decades or two years, you never feel like it was ever enough."

I sat on the arm of the sofa next to him. "There's a piece of my heart that still cries every day." I looked up at the faded coffered ceiling. "I can't be shattered again." I turned my head to hide my tears.

James reached over and placed his hand on my knee. "Listen to me, Elsa. One day you're going to have to come out of your ice castle up in the mountains and spend some time with us peasants." I looked into his aged and caring eyes. "Your heart needs to thaw."

Tears slowly dripped from my face. "For fuck's sake, did you have to reference that movie?" I laughed and wiped my chin. "You know how it makes me a mess."

"Of course I do," he said with a Cheshire smile. "I've taught you well."

AFTER ESCAPING the uniformed confines of Catholic high school, where everyone's worth was based on which model of Range Rover they owned, I'd finally headed off to college, a place I knew was going to change my life forever. I'd thought "change" meant that I would receive a bachelor's in the fine art of bullshit.

Instead it would be the place where I met that ever sought-after prince in disguise.

By the time my junior year came around, I was forced to take an elective and I, like many others, chose a class I knew was going to be a breeze: astronomy. I thought I was going to learn some stuff about the Milky Way, the cosmos, and aliens, but still have time to nap in the back row. The first couple of classes I really tried to pay attention and look interested, but by the end of the class, I was unconscious.

One day in the middle of the semester, I settled into my seat in the back of the room, determined to catch up on the sleep I'd missed the night before because of the *Doctor Who* marathon on

BBC America until four in the morning. I was just about to doze off when the professor asked if anyone had any questions about the upcoming midterm. That sort of question was my usual cue to pass out. Typically no one asked a thing and he would go on his hour-long rant about how NASA didn't know what they were doing half the time. This time, however, someone actually did raise their hand, because Professor McAmbien said, after rustling through his class roster sheet, "Mr. Mathison, correct? What can I help you with?"

Oh great, I thought, *another nerd with a useless question. You know, dude, some of us just want to sleep.*

The nerd in question asked about Orion's Belt. *Bam!* I awoke instantly. Not that I gave a shit about Orion's Belt, shoes, or any other accessory, but I was interested by the deep, sexy drawl I'd just heard come out of my classmate's mouth. I searched the room as the professor, somewhat excitedly, ran to the blackboard and started outlining the significant elements that made up Orion. While he droned on about some nebula or something, I leaned over my desk, scanning the two rows to my left, and if I hadn't caught my pillow—I mean book—in time, I would've tumbled down with it. I sat back too quickly and the chair squeaked, which I thought no one noticed until I made eye contact with the sandy-haired, green-eyed boy wearing cowboy boots. He held my gaze and smiled at me with his pearly whites. I gave him a half-coy, half-*kill me now* smile back and quickly laid my head back down because I was sure I was having a nightmare.

The next class, I went to my usual seat in the back and casually looked around the classroom to see if the Marlboro Man was anywhere to be seen.

"Casually" meaning like a squirrel on crack.

He wasn't there.

Guess it was another of the mental mindfucks my brain liked to play on me. I shook my head to make myself comfortable for my daily nap as the professor rambled on about something to do with Mars. I had just closed my eyes when, to my right, I heard that same voice from the day before.

"'Scuse me," he said. "Mind if I sit here?"

I counted to three and raised my head slowly to make sure I wasn't dreaming. I turned to look up at the boy with the Property of Foster High Athletic Department sweatshirt on and shook my head.

I sat up and pretended to take notes even though I couldn't hear a damn thing the teacher was saying because my blood was pounding in my ears.

"Name's Riley," I heard in a muffled tone.

"Huh?" I so eloquently said back at him. "Oh! Umm, hi. I'm Robbie DeCaro." I stuck out my hand for him to shake, knocking my pen off my desk. "Shit," I whispered as I reached down to grab it.

"I got it," he said as he stretched over his desk too.

I was about to say "It's okay" but was interrupted by our heads crashing together.

You dumb bitch was all I could snap at myself as we both rubbed our now swelling foreheads.

"I'm so fucking sorry," I said to him. "I'm a bit accident-prone."

He just laughed. "Totally cool. Always wanted to get a war wound in astronomy class."

"Yeah, I guess that's better than watching life go by at a glacial pace in here." I smiled at him. "That's why I try to catch up on my beauty rest as much as possible."

He cocked one eyebrow. "It doesn't look like you need much," he said, then gave me a wink that almost made my heart explode.

For the first time in the semester, I sat straight up for the duration of the class and paid attention. Not to the professor, mind you, but to the sweet Southern boy who was as charming as he was handsome.

Weeks after our head-on collision, Riley and I hung out every chance we had and became closer as the months went by. We had absolutely nothing in common, which made our inevitable relationship—and sex life—that much more exciting and interesting. He would fall asleep during one of the many musical movies I subjected him to, while I would ask five dozen times how guys driving around in a circle for three hours was an actual "sport."

Sure, we butted heads—figuratively this time—on certain issues, but somehow it worked and we fell into that gooey mess called love. I took him home to meet my mother and sister one weekend, and they instantly swooned over his Southern accent.

Must be a DeCaro family trait.

Riley's stomach had to endure roughly 300 pounds of pasta and sauce during the many visits we made to my mother's. He would go to the gym to work it off while I could not even look at something edible for a week.

When graduation approached the next year, Riley asked me to move back to Texas with him, and I didn't think twice. My mom still had my sister at home, so she wouldn't be alone, and she always wanted me to be happy. I know inside she didn't want her baby son to leave her, but she would never tell me that. I had only a few close friends I had kept in contact with over the years, so there was nothing really holding me back.

All I wanted was to be with Riley. I had the man of my dreams at my side as we left dreary, brown-tinted Long Island and flew to the mystery land called Foster, Texas, where I could have my long-awaited happily ever after.

Love was something I'd never planned on falling into. I had always told myself that bitch Cupid could wait until I was out on my own, living the glamorous life, schmoozing with Broadway's elite and getting the VIP treatment at Sardi's. I certainly never thought I would move to Texas, of all places. Texas was a state I already thought was ass backward in every way, probably overflowing with people who wouldn't know who Bernadette Peters was if she put on a one-woman version of *Gypsy* right in the middle of the town square that, without a doubt, also doubled as a set from *Hee-Haw*.

For the first time in my life, I knew no one and felt as out of place as that ginger chick with the clamshell bra when she walked on land for the first time. Riley and I stayed in his old bedroom, which by Long Island standards was a deluxe apartment itself, in his parents' house until we could find our own place. Not that I was complaining because during our short time there, I still never saw every floor and wing to the place since I was in constant fear that if I breathed wrong, I would break something. Riley's father, Carl Mathison, came from a long line of oil tycoons—I mean "oil men." Riley told me it wasn't an episode of *Dynasty*, as much I wanted it to be. Anyway, his dad made a very, very decent living from it. His wife and Riley's mother, Dolores, was an elegant but frigid woman who kept to herself most of the time. She did her best to make me feel at home with her ridiculous Southern hospitality. She was like Alexis Carrington's not-as-bitchy sister. Her hair, her clothing, her everything was flawless. So, you see, I got a tiny part of my *Dynasty* fantasy after all.

Riley's two older sisters, who'd married and left the Mathison homestead years ago, were a different story. They were like a really bad episode of *Foster, Texas 90210*. Constantly needing money for manicures and facials and never ever considering the possibility of actually working a day in their lives, they gave the Hilton sisters a run for their money. Luckily I only had to deal with them once—at Riley's and my graduation—because if I had to live with them too, there would've been two new blonde and orange-skinned corpses in the Mathison mausoleum. I think his parents were glad Riley had turned out to be the polite and respectful child they'd dreamed of and not a homeschooled harpy who raided unexpectedly when the moon was in the old gibbous phase. Or the new gibbous phase. Or Friday.

I highly doubted his mom and dad wanted him to like boys, but we all can't get what we want.

When I first met the Mathison clan, Riley didn't exactly introduce me as his boyfriend, but his family was wealthy, not dumb. Riley never gave off the attitude that he was from, as my mother would say, "good stock." He was just that boy who wore beat-up cowboy boots and Foster High alumni gear.

To this day I can only imagine what they thought of the tight-jeaned, obscure designer button-down-shirt-wearing kid who was all googly-eyed over their boy. When Riley called his parents to tell them he was bringing me back with him, I wouldn't doubt they told their various family members and friends that Riley was coming home with a new "roommate" from New York but never went into any further detail. These people were too formal to be bigots. They were just private. Maybe a little ignorant too, but what was I going to do? They were like most of Foster, in fact. The Mathisons could do no wrong because, honestly, they owned half the town. So no one questioned the Mathison boy's new "friend."

One of Riley's cousins, Mabel, was a real estate agent. She found us a cute ranch-style house in town off First Street. Riley, being the one who had majored in finance, got a mortgage very quickly. It didn't hurt to have the last name Mathison, either. I think we also paid it off within the first year. Lord knows that miracle money didn't come from me.

We only stayed at his parents' house for under a month, which was perfectly fine because, as much as I loved being Belle in the Beast's castle, I had issues with people cleaning up after me. I'm quite certain if I'd asked the butler to dress up as a giant candlestick, he would have.

We moved into our new home and got settled quickly. We painted every room and went to the local Hickory Dickory furniture store to buy the majority of their inventory. Riley rarely introduced me to anyone, which was not entirely his fault, because I often ran behind a hanging rack of area rugs or ducked behind the produce display. Being the redneck-fearing person I was, I didn't have the desire to get my head bashed in because I was sleeping with the Mathison heir. If Riley ever thought I was being overdramatic, I never knew. He would just sigh and talk to the salesman himself.

Riley found a job within days due to his degree and family connections. Within a couple of months, he climbed the rather short corporate ladder and was making some nice bucks. I'm sure his good looks, charm, and pedigree helped too. He would come home and tell me about how the girls he graduated high school with still flirted with him. He would laugh it all off, but I secretly wondered if he ever told them about us. Whether people in town knew we were together, I didn't have a clue. I stayed out of their shit and they stayed out of mine. I had no interest in having a one-man gay pride parade down Redneck Street.

As for me, I worked at different temp jobs in offices throughout Foster, always getting weird looks from the hicks because I didn't wear overalls and cowboy boots. Ultimately I got a job in a little thrift shop on the outskirts of town. I was so happy my liberal arts degree was being put to good use. The shop owner, Magda, was a bit eccentric, kooky, and usually smelled like burnt incense. She was different from everyone else I encountered in Foster, and I loved her immediately. She hired me on the spot and said I could start the next morning. It wasn't much pay, but it made me feel like I was contributing something to the household.

Like Magda and that store, I stood on the outside of town looking in.

Sure, I was happy to be there with Riley, but I wasn't convinced I was home.

But who cared that it was a red state and people probably had the IQs of pigeons? Who cared if Texas was 1,700 miles away from everyone and everything I'd known my whole life? This was what I'd been wanting, right?

Fate, quite literally, had bumped me on the head and handed me my sweet prince.

The same prince Fate would one day rip from the world.

And my soul.

Chapter Two
I Don't Know When, I Don't Know How,
But I Want Much More Than This Provincial Life

I WAS ever so slowly trying to readjust myself back to who I was before I left years back. I went food shopping and ran some errands, really doing my best to lead a "normal" life again.

Baby steps.

I opened up my ancient but reliable MacBook. It's amazing how many friends I magically had after I reactivated the Facebook page that had been dormant for half a decade. I got inundated with "likes" and comments from people I hadn't spoken to in forever saying how great it was to have me back and "we should totally hang out!"

Apparently their fingers had been broken this whole time.

I typed "Fuck all y'all" but erased it and wrote a simple "Thanks" instead. What was the point in being pissed at people I frankly hadn't kept in contact with either? You know you do it too. You can have 900 friends on any social media site, but how many of them would you actually care about if they decided to jump off the Empire State building?

My number was in the negative.

The indicator popped up with a red number one saying I had a private message from someone. I clicked on the envelope, thinking it was my mother with another recipe she'd found online for chicken Francese. Instead I was greeted with *Heeeeeey guuuuurl!!!* from my—and I use this term very loosely—friend Sean.

I rolled my eyes not only at the ridiculous spelling of the word "girl" but also because I still possessed a dick as far as I remembered.

Sean was one of those "friends" who was fun to party with but would leave you at a bar once he'd picked a trick for the night. He was a flighty person who would get distracted by a group of assholes he wanted to impress and leave you to fend for yourself against the eighty-year-old trolls who wanted to buy you a drink laced with who-knows-what. I was one of his victims; he left me stranded on Fire Island one year. I ended up having to spend the night on the VD-infested beach. Not one of my stellar moments.

I recall the time Sean invited people to his three-day-long twenty-first birthday party. His "party" spanned four different counties, including a trip to Manhattan, a karaoke bar in Brooklyn, and a sushi lounge in the Hamptons. He also requested that his "friends" help him move to his new apartment in Queens because, and I quote, "It's my birthdaaaaay!" Also, we were told to bring tools because "I don't know how to use them and I just got this *supahcute* vanity from IKEA!"

No, I have no idea why I even bothered either. Maybe he was just a constant reminder of what I never wanted to become. Sean was a self-absorbed queen who got by in life because of his young—and paid for—looks and dippy personality. Apparently it worked in his favor because, according to his Facebook, he now worked as some sort of managerial training person at Tiffany's in the city. That roughly translated to "now he's a bigger egomaniac with a paycheck."

I contemplated erasing the message and not getting involved with Sean's clueless antics when he messaged me again. This time he screeched, *Hiiiieeeee!!! I don't know if you got my last message but I heard that you were baaaaaack!!!*

Why was he shouting so much?

I sighed, knowing that if I didn't answer him I was going to be subjected to more elongated rape of the English language because he typed the way he spoke. *Hey, Sean*, I wrote. *Yes, I'm back on Long Island. How are you?* I knew I shouldn't have asked because number one, I didn't really care and number two, I really didn't want to hear about how *fabulous* his life was when I was in the process of resuscitating mine.

OMG! I'M AMAAAAZING!!! You have to come to city and see the view from my office! It's STUNNING! And OMG, you have to meet my new boyfriend, Rinaldo. He's Puerto Riiiiicaaaan and GURL my ass is throbbing just thinking of him right NOW!!!

Nope. I didn't need to hear any of that.

Aww... that's nice :) was all I could muster because I knew it would satisfy his craving for attention and stop him from going on any more about his supposedly fascinating life.

But how are YOU?! he wrote back. *Are you still with that cowboy??? Ride 'im, partner!!!!*

That one sentence punched all the air out of my body while the cursor blinked on the screen. My hands dropped from hovering above the keyboard as a gamut of emotions including anger, sadness, and most of all, pain, coursed through my veins.

I shouldn't have been surprised that Sean, let alone the rest of my supposed friends, didn't know about Riley. I wasn't the type of person to write a status message of everything I was feeling at any given moment of the day.

Look at my adorable puppy!

Glee *is the worst. Show. Ever.*

I just took a shit that looks like Jesus.

I wasn't one to write *Hey, everyone! My boyfriend just died. #sad.* It just wasn't me. My business was my business, and no one needed to hear the constant torture my mind and body were being put through at the time.

The pop-up sound beeped. *You there?????* Sean wrote.

Yeah, sorry, I typed. *Phone rang.*

NP. So you still with him???

I took a deep breath and simply wrote *No.* There was no reason to give a full explanation to someone who thought the universe revolved around his suntanned world.

Ok good because there's a new bar that just opened up this week and I'm dyyyyyiiing to goooo....

I was part relieved and part pissed that he didn't ask why I wasn't with Riley anymore, but again, this was a selfish person who didn't know any better. Plus I knew that him telling me a new bar opened this week translated to "I want to go to this bar and get completely fucked up so you have to drive because we all know how you won't meet anyone."

Unfortunately, it was the truth.

My even opening up Facebook was the only thing social, outside of shopping with my mother and sister or hanging out at James's house, I'd done in the past couple of weeks. I knew I had to reestablish myself in society before I adopted twenty-two cats and ate cans of frosting by the case.

However, I wasn't going to jump so easily into the kind of trap Sean set when we used to go out clubbing together. *Where is it and when do you want to meet there?*

I could almost hear his heart drop when he realized he couldn't be a drunken whore for the night. *Umm.... Well, it's called Thunders and it's in Huntington across from Stop N Shop. Let's meet at 11 on Friday??*

I quickly went through the Google map of my mind and remembered the grocery store I used to work at when I was in high school. Huntington was an uppity area of Long Island, but it was a gay bar. There wouldn't be judgmental pretty boys just hanging around judging me, right? That *never* happens in the gay community ever.

Yeah, who am I kidding?

Sounds good, I responded. *I'll see you there.*

YAAAAAAYYYYAYYY!!!!!! Sean screamtyped. *CAN'T WAIT!!!!!!!*

Somehow I didn't mind waiting.

AFTER A few months of living in Foster, I'd started to feel like Riley and I were the only two gay people in the godforsaken town. I had no one to talk to. Magda was great company and all, but I needed some people who were like me to converse with. Well, besides the teenaged girls who came in that I would discuss the latest episode of *Gossip Girl* with. Since Riley had learned how to read my mind and could sense how out of my element I was, one night he told me to get cleaned up and dressed because he was going to take me out to a place where I could let loose. I gave him a distrustful stare but did as he asked.

We drove out of town for at least thirty-five minutes to a shack of a building I swear could've been a filming location for the next *Saw* movie. The parking lot was almost full but Riley found a spot in the back. When I opened the car door, I felt the bass of the speakers from where I stood.

My smile could have lit up the night sky. He came up from behind me and grabbed my hand, pulling me toward the front door. When it opened, there were men—and about three ladies— all milling about in what I assumed was the only gay bar this part of Texas had ever seen. The place wasn't exactly the first gay bar I'd been to but I didn't give three shits. I took a deep breath and finally felt like I belonged.

As we walked in, someone said, "Hey, boys!" and we turned around. A bright flash stunned the both of us, and a large man started laughing.

"Yup," he said as he looked at the digital camera, "that's a keeper!"

Riley snickered while I gave the photographer a nasty look.

"Oh, don't you look at me like that, Missy," he responded to my face's expression. "It's a tradition here." He pointed to a wall of photos that started out with Polaroids, then 35 mm, and finally digitally colored. Each picture was of one, occasionally two, boys or men. Each person was unique, but the shocked expressions on their faces were virtually identical.

"I'm Tom," the burly man said, "and welcome to the Bear's Den." He grinned like a pig in shit, and I just shook my head. Riley was still having a laughing fit. "C'mon, Miss Thing," Tom added as he put his arm around me. "I'll buy you your first drink."

I looked back at Riley, who just shrugged when I gave him a *You're not getting any for a month* glare.

"What'll you have?" Tom asked.

"Umm…." I stammered, "a dirty martini?"

"Is that your final answer?" Tom said.

I nodded.

"Scott?" Tom called to the bartender. "Get my friend— what's your name, sweetcheeks?"

"Robbie?" I answered uncertainly.

"Get Robbie here a dirty martini. Use the Goose and don't be stingy." The bartender nodded.

"You really don't have to do that," I said, a little weirded out.

"I want to," Tom replied. "And don't worry, I'm not hitting on you. You're a little too skinny and young for me." He chuckled.

I laughed back because I didn't know what else to do and said, "But isn't that kind of expensive?"

"Like I give a rat's ass," Tom laughed. "I own the place, so I can give whoever I want whatever I want. No, not you, John. Go back to milking that Bud Light you started three hours ago. Don't think I'm not watching you." He turned his head to a guy sitting on a barstool on his left and looking completely scared.

Riley sat next to me, and Tom ordered him a Corona. I shouldn't be surprised he picked Riley's favorite beer. It was a 50/50 shot since Texas seemed to only import Corona and Bud Light. They both tasted like piss water.

"So, not from around here, are ya?" Tom asked me as I took a big gulp of my drink.

I shook my head.

"This here is your boyfriend, I'm assuming?"

"Yup," I said. "This is Riley."

"Pleasure, Riley," and Tom tipped his imaginary hat.

"Quite a place you got here," I said to Tom after my drink was halfway done and I felt more relaxed. Scott certainly wasn't stingy with the vodka.

"Sure is," Tom said proudly. "Only gay bar around here for miles."

"Well, at least there is one," I said. "I thought I was going to have to open one right in my own living room." I laughed at my joke. Damn, that drink was good.

"It's not much," Tom admitted, "but at least it's somewhere we can all be ourselves."

I smiled at him because that's exactly what I needed to hear. I looked around and besides the rainbow flags and disco balls, I saw a wall full of news clippings and other pictures very different than the one Tom took of me and Riley. "What's all that?" I asked him.

Tom frowned. "That's our memory wall. It's something to keep us all in check."

"What do you mean?" I asked, even more intrigued.

"Over there you will see obituaries, funeral notices, and pictures of the ones we lost."

"Kinda morbid, don't you think?" I hoped I wouldn't offend him.

"It is but it isn't," Tom didn't seem the least bit offended. I'm sure I wasn't the first person to say it. "It's a reminder of the battle we still have to fight in this fucked-up world. Those people died from being beaten, shot, or because of AIDS. We can't forget the battle isn't over." Tom stared pensively at the bar.

I put my hand on his shoulder, and in that moment I knew I'd just made a great friend. What I didn't know was how much that wall was going to mean to me in the near future.

We stayed all night and even helped Tom clean up after the crowd left. All three of us joked around until the sun came up. We said our good-byes with big hugs and told Tom we would be back.

And we were. Every Friday and Saturday night for months, Riley and I went to the Bear's Den. Sometimes I would go by myself, and Tom was right there in case some scumbag tried to hit on me to let the asshole know I was taken. Of course, I could've defended myself with my razor tongue, but having a 300-pound bearded man telling you to "Keep your fucking paws off the merchandise" carried more weight.

Literally.

I GOT out of the shower, checked the clock on my phone, and saw that it was 10:54. I just finished drying off when the text message sound went off. The inevitable message from Sean was blinking on the screen.

HEEEEEY!!! SORRY!!! I'm a scoach lateeeee. Shuld b there in 15!!!!

I put down the phone and continued to get dressed. I knew he was going to be late because nothing had changed since the last time I saw him. Sean Time was something I had gotten used to whenever we went out. He was a shit, but he was the closest thing I had to a friend my age here.

Foster had been, at times, boring and outright painful, but in the end, I left knowing I had real friends there that I would love forever.

When I packed up my life and left Long Island with Riley, I had never felt that way.

I was a shy, quiet, somewhat cute twink back when I started my big gay adventure, but not the one anyone ever paid attention to. I wasn't baby-faced and I refused to shave every single piece of body hair. I was ignored by one guy to the next whenever I went out to a bar. I barely had any friends, let alone anyone who was willing to date me.

You thought I was always the outspoken bitch you know today? Not so much. I was a complete social disaster.

The only other gay person around my age I had any sort of "friendship" with was Sean. He was one of those people who would come flitting into your life whenever everyone else who was better looking than you wouldn't return his phone calls and you were the last person in his contact list.

"Hey, guuurl!" he would squeal when I regretfully answered my phone. "We should totes check out that new bar on the Island tonight!"

The "Island" was short for Fire Island, where I would go to feel even less attractive than I already was.

Muscled, tanned bodies covered in glitter with white powder coming out of their noses.

I fit in perfectly.

Please repeat that with sarcasm.

I would go regardless because I had nothing better to do once I finished reading my weekly comics. We would stand at the bar until Sean found somebody better to talk to and left me. I didn't blame him. I was the gay nerd, or g'nerd for short, standing there milking a strawberry daiquiri. And it wasn't like he was a bad-looking person with his forever tanned skin and swimmer's physique.

I secretly hated him even more than I care to admit. He was annoying but knew his looks would get him anyone he wanted.

And believe me, they did. I wouldn't be surprised if his ass doubled as the Lincoln Tunnel when he wasn't out at a bar looking for a new trick.

I had no idea why I constantly put myself through that. Sean really was a shit and would constantly tell me that I needed to hit the gym and lie out in the sun if I was ever going to score a "quality" man. The only thing I wanted to "hit and tan" was his little cherub face with the back of my hand. I never had and never would go to a gym unless they started doing Jazzercise classes again and I could break out the legwarmers I made my mother buy me when I was young and totally obsessed with Olivia Newton-John.

After a while, Mr. Grey Goose slowly became the only friend I liked hanging out with and the only friend who gave me the courage to talk to guys. I remember the last trip I took to the Island with Sean. I got so trashed that I finally had the balls to flirt with this hot Greek-god-looking guy dancing on the bar. I think I slurred something ridiculous like "You come here often?" to him, at which he completely ignored me or couldn't hear me over the bass of the speakers. When I tried to talk to him again, I felt the chunks rising up in my throat and ran to the bathroom to puke. By the time I came out after throwing up everything I'd ever eaten, Sean was on top of the bar making out with Mr. Greek Fire Island.

I was pissed. I had no idea why, but I wanted to crack a bottle on the bar and shove it in Sean's face like they did in those dramas on TV. The guy he was sloppily making out with wasn't my boyfriend or anything, but something about the whole situation made me furious. For all I knew, Sean had been watching me make a fool of myself on the sidelines and waiting for the perfect time to pounce.

I didn't know it then, but now I've come to realize that I was angrier at myself than I was at him. I'd done this to myself and hung out with Sean for my own selfish reasons, thinking maybe he would throw me a leftover once in a while. But that night I was done playing the wallflower while party boys like him had all the fun.

Don't get me wrong, I wasn't planning on tweeking out on E or anything, but I knew I didn't want to sit and watch my life go by on fast-forward.

I took the next ferry back to Sayville and sat on top of the boat so the cool night air would sober me up faster. I drove the twenty minutes home, leaving Sean to find his own way back to the mainland.

I had no idea what happened to him after that night, because I hadn't heard from him again until this week. Whether he was pissed I left him stranded on Fire Island or too busy getting plowed by a go-go boy or finally forgot my number, I couldn't tell you. Even though he was a toxic son of a bitch, I was glad I'd met Sean, because he showed me what kind of person I should never become.

Yet here I was, years later, getting dressed to go hang out with him at some lame Long Island bar.

How sad was it that I missed sassy, blond emo teenagers?

It was after 11:30 by the time I put the final touches on my outfit for the evening. Which meant I put on a hat because I didn't feel like doing anything with my hair. It went well with the worn jeans and *Doctor Who* shirt I was sporting.

Don't look at me like that. This was the opening of a gay bar in Long Island, not the red carpet at the Oscars. If the night went the way I thought it would, half the men, whether they had business to or not, would be half-naked and making out with each other by 1:00 a.m.

About halfway to the bar, I got a text from Sean asking where I was.

Actually it was more like, *WHEEERRREEEHHH AAAREE UUUU??? IM DRUUUNK!!!*

I didn't even bother responding because I was sure he was about to drink tequila shot number eight at the moment.

I pulled into the crowded parking lot. The bass from the speakers inside was vibrating my rearview mirror like the Tyrannosaurus scene in *Jurassic Park*. I looked at my reflection and rehearsed my signature fake smile for when it was needed. I wasn't looking to impress anyone, but I didn't want them to turn to stone if they looked directly into my bitter eyes. I took a deep breath, got out of the car, and beeped the alarm.

The air had a certain greasy smell to it that brought back the feelings of nervousness and excitement in the middle of my chest I'd felt when I first went to the Bear's Den forever ago. Tom's food would clog your arteries, but damn, it was good. Tonight the scent was coming from the practically empty diner across the street. In a few hours, that diner would be full to capacity with drunk people demanding cheese fries and brown gravy.

Just like when I was back in Texas, standing outside the Bear's Den, I had no idea what to expect inside the bar.

What was worse was that I was all alone.

I got to the door, opened it, and walked inside to the bouncer, who was checking IDs of the people in front of me. He was a burly black man with a baseball hat and a face that looked like it wanted to be anywhere but there.

I reached into my pocket to get my license out when he waved me through.

"But don't you want to see this?" I asked as I held up the card.

He looked me up and down. "Nah, you're good," he said and motioned for the person behind me to come to him.

Ouch.

I know I'm not twenty-one, but I'm not exactly eighty either. When someone asks for your ID, whether you're buying alcohol or cigarettes at the local 7-Eleven, it makes you feel young and innocent again.

Strike one against my ego for the night.

The bar was packed like a rainbow-colored sardine can, with people laughing and dancing on top of any flat surface available. I looked right and left for any sign of a glitter cloud named Sean but with no luck. I gave up after five minutes and decided to go to the endless line at the bar for a drink. Some guys were pounding beers and cheering one of their friends on to chug his Corona Light.

"Yeah, take it all in, man!" one Neanderthal yelled out. "The only way to get over him is to get *blitzed*!" His friends screamed louder in response, and I tried to move closer to the bar and away from these assholes in case they decided to break something, namely me.

Since when did a Long Island gay bar turn into a frat house kegger? I asked myself. I shook my head and finally made it to the bartender. He was a beefy guy wearing only briefs and sneakers. I smiled and loudly asked for a Grey Goose dirty martini.

The bartender nodded and quickly started to assemble my order. While I was waiting, I turned back to the crowd and saw the group of guys pumping their fists in the air like they were on the new season of *Jersey Shore*. Did they know where they were?

Before my eyes rolled any further, I felt a tap on my shoulder. The bartender put the drink down in front of me. He stuck one finger up with his right hand and four fingers with his left.

"Fourteen dollars?" I asked and he nodded. I shook my head, not used to paying so much for a drink.

I handed him a twenty, which he grabbed out of my hand, almost giving me a paper cut. He rang up the drink and proceeded to help a customer at the other end of the bar.

"You're welcome!" I yelled, but he either didn't hear or just didn't give a shit.

I took a sip of my drink and almost spit it right back in the glass. It tasted like warm water with a hint of vodka and way too much olive juice. I took another sip and gagged. The second gulp wasn't any better. I ate the one fourteen-dollar olive and put the glass back on the bar.

I was about to flag the bartender down when I heard a high-pitched squeal from my left.

"Oh. My. *Gahhdd*! You made it!" a familiar voice wailed as a human wall lumbered toward me and sloppily hugged me.

I pushed the mass away and tried to identify who stood in front of me.

"Sean?" I ventured.

"Of course, giiiirl!" he said and whacked me on the shoulder. "Who did you think I was? Joan Crawford?"

I took a step back to look at him. The years had certainly changed Sean. He was a little bulkier than he used to be. I mean, it looked like he'd been working out, but the bloated stomach made it seem like he'd had some unnatural "help" along the way.

"Wow! You look great!" I lied, fake smile firmly Krazy Glued to my lips.

"Thaaaank you!" he said and gave me a once-over. "And you look…." He paused. "Just like you!"

Ego hit, strike two.

"Thanks. I guess," I responded with the least amount of venom possible.

"OMG! Come meet my friends!" Sean grabbed my hand and almost ripped my arm out of its socket as he dragged me to the group of schmucks I'd been avoiding most of the night. I assumed Sean was working off a different definition of "friend" than the rest of us were used to. Where *friend* to most meant people you know, trust, and like, here it meant people who would drink and make him look pretty.

Oh, great, I thought as we got closer.

"Hey, everybody!" Sean yelled, and the herd looked over at us. "This is Robbie! My best friend in the entire universe!"

I was right; he was using a custom version of the word *friend*. I looked at Sean like he just grew a new set of arms. *Best friend?* I thought, terrified at what being Sean's any kind of friend might mean. Where the fuck had that come from? I took a deep breath and realized the words were spoken by Jose Cuervo and not Sean. I turned to smile at his friends.

Now, I've given and have been witness to many judgmental looks, but theirs took the cake. It was like the *Attack of the Clones* and all of them mind-melded together for one vaporizing stare. I was nothing but a speck on the ground beneath their A&F-clad feet. Just like that, I was back on Fire Island feeling less than human, except this time I wasn't blitzed out of my mind to ease the pain. It was like being in high school if you attended WB High. I could hear the voiceover now. "This week a new face in the halls turns heads. But not in a good way."

For once in his life, Sean had good timing and whipped me around, avoiding any more judginess. "I'm so happy you're here! You get to meet my new boyfriend!" If he wasn't so heavy, he would've been jumping up and down like a schoolgirl.

"Oh," I said weakly, "a new one? Is it that Latino guy you've been dating?"

"Who?" Sean asked quite innocently.

"Never mind," I said.

"Anyway. My new boy's sooo hot! And sweet!" Sean looked like he was about to pop from the excitement. "I was lucky to hook him too. These cows have been trying to get on his dick all night!" A couple of the guys shot a glance at Sean. "Hehehe! Just kidding y'all!" He winked at them. "They're soooo jealous!" he whispered in my ear.

I smiled the best I could and nodded. "So what's his name?"

"Who?" Sean asked while ordering another drink.

"Umm... your boyfriend?" I said.

"Oh! Silly me!" Sean knocked on his head like it was empty. Which it was, by the way. "Umm.... John? No, wait. Dennis?"

I stared at him. "Wait a sec. He's your boyfriend and you don't know his name?"

"Of course I do, you mess! It just escaped me for a minute!" he screamed back.

"How long have you been together?" I asked.

"Umm… like a half hour?" Sean said nonchalantly.

"What?" I yelled at him, and he jumped. "You can't be boyfriends with someone you just met!"

"Like hell I can!" he spat back. "Not all of us can be uptight hard-asses like you waiting for 'the one'!"

If he had picked up a barstool and rammed it into my stomach, it would not have hurt as much as what he had just said.

I swallowed back the tears that were forming in my eyes and smiled at him, pretending not to be hurt. "I have to use the bathroom," I said to him and turned before he could see me cry.

"If you see my boyfriend in there, tell him I'm waaaaiting!" he called to the back of my head.

I pushed the door open and almost knocked over two guys who were making out hardcore next to the stalls. I went to the farthest sink and turned on the cold water. I splashed my face and moved close to the mirror since the lighting was so dim. I understood that fluorescent lighting was a gay man's archnemesis, but how the hell were drag queens going to do touch-ups or thirty-year-old men look at their pathetic selves without enough luminescence to see by?

As I dried off my face, in the mirror I saw a guy practically fall out of a stall and come bumbling toward me.

"Move!" he bellowed. He pushed me out of the way of the sink and stuck his head under the faucet.

"Dude!" I yelled. "Watch it! You almost knocked me over!"

He was lapping the water up like dog and gave me a sideways look. He took a breath of air while the water was still splashing his face. "Drunk you! I'm fuck!" he said and went back to drinking whatever liquid might pass as tap water in a club.

"Typical," I said. "Nothing has changed in this fucking place. All you guys are still fucking assholes. I knew I should've stayed home."

He lifted his head to say something to me, but since it was so dark and he was forty-five sheets to the wind, he didn't notice the puddle of water under him and slipped and fell onto his stomach, which of course, in turn, made him vomit all over the bottom half of my legs.

"*Are you fucking kidding me?*" I screamed. "I'm fucking done!" I shook off what puke I could and talked to the person lying in a puddle of gross below me. "And thank you for ruining an already fucked-up night, you fucking dumbass!"

He looked up at me for a second and then cocked his head. "I don't get it. Doctor Who?"

"It's a TV show!" I shot back.

"Really? You wore a shirt from a TV show to a club? What are you, twelve?"

Ego strike three.

I stepped over him and ran out of the bathroom and the club to my car. I unlocked it but, before I sat, I looked down at my soaking pants and shoes. As much as my car has been bumped and bruised, it didn't deserve to smell like a dirty bedpan.

I checked to see if anyone was looking and sat down on the driver's seat without getting my dirty pants or Converses inside the car. I took off the shoes and put them on the ground. I took everything out of my pockets and slowly peeled my jeans off. I used them to wipe the rest of the vomit off my sneakers and threw them in front of the passenger seat. I rolled up my now ruined pants and chucked them into the nearest bush. It wouldn't be the first time someone lost their pants in the parking lot of a gay bar.

I closed the door and drove home in my socks and tighty-whities. I silently prayed to the gods that I wouldn't be pulled over for any reason and have to explain to the poor officer where the fuck my pants were.

Luckily no cops were out. I pulled into my driveway, grabbed my shoes and wallet, and walked to the back of my mother's house. I slowly picked my way over the endless stones surrounding the pool and up to my front door. I slammed it behind me and fell to the floor, crying.

I thought I was done crying over myself. I thought things were finally going to be different. I thought the years would've changed this place.

My thoughts were wrong. I was wrong. It was all the same.

I don't know long I cried, and I don't know when sleep finally came to my rescue.

AS WE were driving to the bar one summer night, Riley told me he'd run into an old friend from school earlier in the day and had invited him out with us that night.

"Wait a minute," I said. "There's another gay man in town who isn't a creepy florist? And you're just telling me about him now?"

Riley's eyes stayed on the road but his cheeks turned a little red. "I haven't mentioned anything because he just recently came out, and I know how you can get."

"Excuse me?" I replied with some venom. "How can I 'get,' pray tell?"

"Well," he started slowly, "you can come off a little strong, and that's not a bad thing, but Tyler is very quiet, and he's still trying to figure everything out."

I stared at the side of Riley's face and cocked an eyebrow. "In other words he's a newbie and you're afraid I might barf a rainbow all over his face." In Riley's defense, I suppose I did come across like a one-man Broadway show sometimes.

Riley shook his head. "That's not what I meant. Please don't be upset with me," he added hastily. He always hated confrontation and would literally leave the room if two people were arguing in front of him. "Just take it easy on him is all I'm asking."

"Fine." I sighed dramatically. "I'll be a good boy and make nice."

He looked over at me after he parked the car. "Thank you," he said with kiss on my forehead.

"Yeah, yeah," I sighed.

"I think that's his car," he said as he pointed to a sedan across the way.

"That looks like it's about to leave," I said, noticing the car slowly inching toward the exit with its headlights on.

Riley waved at the car, and it stopped abruptly. The driver whacked his hand on the steering wheel, no doubt pissed that he'd been caught.

"Oh, this is going to be fun," I muttered under my breath as I got out of the car. Luckily Riley didn't hear me because he was on his way to the failed escapee's vehicle. I closed the door and walked over to meet my boyfriend's BFF.

Riley's friend got out of his car, and I stopped in my tracks.

"You've *got* to be kidding me," I whispered to myself.

I'd seen this guy in town before, and I'd had to prevent myself from staring at him a couple of times. He was fucking hot and I wasn't afraid to admit it. Tall, blond, and built a little bigger than Riley.

Look, I loved my Riley, but I wouldn't be honest with you if I said I never gazed upon the very rare pretty things in Foster. I think this guy worked at the sporting goods place around the corner from my store, so it was hard not to see him practically every day.

I shook myself out of my fog and walked up behind Riley.

"You were going to chicken out, right?" Riley asked as his friend slammed the car door shut. "You were just thinking about burning rubber out of here like a little girl."

"Shut up" was all the response Riley got.

How cute. Hot guy banter. Could I feel any more like the ugly girl at a party?

"Right," Riley said, stifling a laugh. "So, Tyler, this is my partner, Robbie."

God, I hate that word. It's the equivalent of "significant other." A dog is a significant other to me. Riley and I weren't in the coal business together, so the term "partner" rubbed me the wrong way. "I'm your fucking *boyfriend*" was about to come out of my mouth, but I bit my tongue when he reached for my hand behind him.

"Robbie, this is Tyler." Riley smiled at the both of us.

"Hi," the golden boy said, extending his hand. "I'm Tyler. I went to school with Riley."

I stared at him and took his hand. "Of course you did," I answered, deadpan.

Confused, he looked at Riley, who was shaking his head and laughing. "Robbie is under the impression they put something in the water around here," Riley explained.

I whacked him in the chest and stared back at Tyler. "I'm serious," I said. "It's like a goddamned Abercrombie & Fitch commercial around here. Were there any normal-looking guys who went to school with you?"

"Um… yes?" Mr. November said sheepishly.

Christ, he was hot and dumb. Perfect.

"It's no wonder half of you are freakin' gay," I grumbled before stomping off toward the bar. "You guys look like you're all underwear models on a break!" I yelled back at them and, not wanting to hear any more hot boy talk, swung open the bar door. Guess I'd failed the only job I had in the "being nice tonight" department.

Oh fucking well.

The door shut behind me as the pulsing music hit my ears. I waved at Tom, who was behind the bar, and yelled, "Incoming!"

Tom smiled and ran to grab his camera. I pulled up a barstool and ordered a drink while I waited for the boys to come in. Riley held the door for Tyler and, when the flash went off, the guy looked like he was going to kill someone. I almost fell off my chair because I was laughing so hard. Riley came over and sat down next to me. Tom extended his hand to Tyler. "You just have to shake it, not kiss it," Tom said after thirty seconds of waiting. Tyler shook his hand like he was dying, but he listened when Tom explained why he took the picture. "So, you see, it's tradition."

Tyler didn't seem at all pleased and looked like he was about to try to wrestle Tom's camera away from him.

I would've loved to see him try.

Tom put his hand on Tyler's shoulder, and he looked at Tom's paw like it was covered in pus. Unfazed, Tom walked him over to the bar. "What it'll be, Tyler?" Tom asked.

"Nothing," Tyler said.

"Oh, you must want something to calm that cute ass of yours," Tom said with a wink.

Tyler looked mortified.

"Don't pay attention to *her*, Tyler," I said with a laugh. "He does that with everyone. He's such a whore sometimes."

"Only on days that end in Y, sweet pea!" Tom chuckled.

Tom, Riley, and I laughed. Tyler stood there in silence.

"I think he needs a beer, Tom," I said after I controlled my laughter.

Tom reached over the counter, grabbed a Heineken, and handed it to Tyler. "Drink this," Tom said. "We'll all look better when you're done."

"I look fabulous sober!" I said to Tom, flipping my imaginary weave.

"I'm glad you think so," Tom said and stuck out his tongue. We both cackled, and Riley shook his head but laughed quietly.

Tyler downed his beer in ten seconds flat.

"Dude," I said to him, "I hope you're not planning on driving."

Tyler swallowed his last gulp. "Yeah, why?"

"Well, you'll be rolling back home if you don't slow down," I warned him.

"Sorry," Tyler said, "It's just that this is my first time at a...." He lowered his voice. "You know."

"Why are you whispering? Is someone asleep?" I said. "Yes, you are at a *gay bar*!" I shouted, making Tyler jump and maybe two people look over at me. "See? No one cares." I motioned with my hand.

"Yeah, but no one knows I'm gay," he said with a look of shame.

"Ah," I said, "that explains it. Your secret is safe with me and the fifty other people in here." I crossed my heart.

"Can I have another beer?" Tyler asked Tom.

"Sure you can," Tom said. "But this time it'll be five bucks."

Tyler pulled out a five and two singles and gave it to Scott, who was ready with another beer.

Tom handed over the beer but stopped suddenly. "You're the Parker boy who runs the sporting goods place up in town, aren't ya?"

Tyler turned pale but nodded.

"I thought I recognized you from the newspaper," Tom said and gave Tyler the beer. "Weren't you a big-time football star in Florida?"

"I was," Tyler said after a sip, "but I busted my knee, so now I'm back, and I run the family store ever since my parents retired."

"And this is why I don't do sports," I chimed in. "Sitting on my ass watching reruns of *Charmed* won't get me hurt." I giggled. "This one over here does all the working out for the both of us." I pointed with my thumb at Riley.

Tyler smiled. Looks like I—or the alcohol—had chipped some of his fear away.

"You're funny," Tyler said.

"Thank you. I already knew that," I said with some sass. "Kidding! But not really, I'm hilarious."

Everyone laughed, including Tyler. He stayed for another beer, catching up with Riley.

I stared at probably two of the hottest guys I'd seen in my life.

I slowly sipped my martini, quietly waiting for the part when Riley would turn to me and say, "So now that I definitely know my hot high school buddy likes dick, I'm dumping your skinny ass for him. You can get a ride back to Long Island, right?"

Fortunately that never happened because Tyler said he had to go. He had to open the shop at 10:00 a.m. And it was already past one.

"Will we see you again?" Tom asked as Tyler got off his barstool.

"I think so," Tyler replied with a smile. "Thank you all for the fun." He looked at me. "And the laughs."

"Any time," I said to him and gave him a hug. His body went stiff, and I let go. "I'm a hugger. Get over it. I'm practically married." I gave his cheek a squeeze half like a grandmother and half like a semijealous boyfriend letting him know I could squeeze other parts of the body until they fell off. "Get home safe now, got it?"

"I will," he said with a brilliant smile; and he left the building.

I pinched Riley on the arm. "See? I told you I can be nice when I want to be."

He just rolled his eyes and kissed me.

Tyler, Riley, and I became closer as the weeks went by. I tried to explain the differences between a soundtrack and an original cast recording to Tyler while Riley sat back and enjoyed the show. My rainbow vomit spewed more and more, and Tyler got more and more confused.

Other than my weekly lessons in all things fabulous, we hung out at the Bear's Den a couple of nights a week and would ask Tyler to join us. He would usually say yes, but at other times he wouldn't go without a fight.

"You do know you aren't getting any younger, right?" I said to Tyler when he tried to make an excuse for not going out one night. "You're, like, a couple of years away from your body realizing it's midnight. Then, trust me, you're going to wish you had used what you had when you had it." My mind flashed with an image of Tyler trying on glass slippers.

He gave me a wry yet sexy grin. "And what exactly do I have?"

It took all my strength not smack him Cher-style across the face. "Fuck you, I am not feeding that already Godzilla-like ego you possess. Stay here and get old. We are going out."

He gave in eventually, like he always did, and followed us to our car, but not without saying, "No. Come on, tell me what I have now! I want to hear you say it."

"I hate this town," I mumbled to Riley for the eighty-fifth time that week before slamming the car door behind me. It was like being in the Chelsea part of New York City with these two.

Riley, like me, needed someone in his life whom he could talk to about his interests and who wasn't "on fire" like I was most every day. He could've used a friend who didn't care about the Tonys as much as I did. I understood that, but it didn't stop my self-confidence from running to the nearest exit whenever Tyler and he shared an inside joke, especially about some guy they had gone to school with and had a secret crush on. I imagined which page of *GQ* or *Bait 'n' Tackle* the boy in question walked out of. It was like the years they hadn't spoken were nothing. They'd chat about random sport-type things while I nodded every so often when I recognized a familiar phrase. "Tight end" was the one that usually got my attention for some reason.

I knew there was a part of Tyler that desperately wanted a Riley of his own. But I'd be goddamned if he ever took mine. I honestly didn't mind them talking. The thing about Tyler that always got under my skin was that he didn't want to hang out unless Riley was there. And it wasn't like I didn't try, either. One time I texted him to see if he wanted to go to Nancy's, the cute— and only—diner in town, because I was in the mood for cheese fries. He asked if Riley was going to be there, and I said no because he was working. After about five seconds of dead air, Tyler told me some customers had just happened to walk in at that very minute, and he couldn't make it. I knew it was a bunch of horseshit because I could see the front of his store from the windows of mine.

That wasn't the first, second, or third time Tyler disappointed me. And it certainly wasn't going to be the last.

A WEEK had passed since the last time I had heard from Sean, and that was only a drunk text he sent at three in the morning the night I'd gone to the bar, asking, "GUUUURRRLLL…. WHHEERREERD YU GOIO?@!"

I didn't bother replying because there was no point. Sean had proved that night he was no better than the person I'd first encountered years back. He got with someone as soon as he met them and dropped any other relationships he had. While I was seriously lacking in the friend department since I'd come back home, I didn't need to be in contact with someone like him.

I really didn't want to admit that I missed Foster, since I'd finally gotten the smell of hay out of my clothing, but I missed the band of musketeers I'd called friends, no, family there. Kyle and Brad, my "adopted" children—for lack of a better term, and more on that later—were trying to make it out west in California while Tom, Tyler, Linda, and that dum-dum Matt still moseyed around in their horse and buggies in good ol' Foster, Texas.

In Foster I was the outcast, the witch who lived atop a lonely mountain in a two-bedroom house. I would fly down on my broom to hang out with the only people I considered friends whenever I could, but also to terrorize the munchkin community of Foster.

Terrorizing the older munchkins was especially delightful.

Most people saw me as the freak who ran the secondhand store in town. In their eyes I'd taken over for the older freak who had opened it in the first place. I reveled in their fears, masking myself in the character I'd created and forcing them to stay as far away as possible.

I was so bitter and bruised that it took a team of gay men, former alcoholics, and teenage boys to get me out of the depression I had been in for so long. Believe me, it wasn't done overnight, nor was it easy for any of us. I'll tell you the stories when I've got time, and you may wonder what the hell was wrong with me.

A month had gone by since the dreaded bar fiasco, and I still was doing my daily routine of checking e-mails, going food shopping, and hanging with my family. Uncle James would stop over every so often to have a cup of coffee with my mom and me. I knew having coffee was an excuse to get out of his house and not clean it. I saw random people I'd gone to high school with wherever I went, and we exchanged phone numbers or Facebook names, but we all knew nothing was going to come of it other than taking up space in our contact lists. It was summertime, and I worked on my little garden outside my front door, trying to keep everything from wilting in the ninety-degree heat.

I was weeding my lonely tomato plant when my pocket started to vibrate and Katy Perry's "Roar" played.

"My darling sister," I said when I answered. "To what do I owe the pleasure? It's two in the afternoon, so I'm sure you're not drunk enough to need me to pick you up."

Back when we were younger, Nicole would call at all times of the night begging for a ride home because she'd gone out to a bar and partied until she puked. I'm not sure how she got by when I moved away.

"Number one, you're an asshole," she responded. "Number two, it's only Monday. I have to have a full week in this hellhole before I have enough reason to drink until my liver cries out in pain." At least she had priorities. "Number three, and I hope you're sitting down for this, there's this really supahcute guy who just started working here, and it turns out he's gay, soooo I gave him your number. You're welcome."

I almost dropped the phone and got into my car to go hunt her down.

"I'm going to fucking kill you," I hissed into the receiver and went into the house to get out of the heat.

"What?" she responded innocently. "I didn't do anything wrong." I could almost hear her bat her eyelashes like a baby deer.

"Yes, you did. You gave some random guy my phone number without telling me!" I paced around my living room, wanting to throw something.

"I did tell you!" she screeched back.

"Yeah, just *now*, Nic! What the fuck were you thinking?" I started breathing heavily and knew an anxiety attack was just waiting around the corner to jump me. "How do you even know he's gay and not some guy who was pretending to be so he can 'experiment' with me?" I've seen those dumb movies before.

"Oh, stop being so dramatic. You sound like Ma." My eyes tried to fry her face through the phone. "He works in the mail room here," she explained, like mailmen were a secret fetish of mine or something. "And believe me, he's gay. Don't think I didn't flirt hardcore with him when I met him." Small pause. "Not for me, of course, but to make sure."

Allow me to introduce you to my sister, Nicole. She's what my dearly departed grandmother called "a piece of work." She's a beautiful woman who could have—and has had—her share of any guy she wants, but she's not some pretty face who hooks up with just random dumb guys.

No, you see, my sister is also one of the smartest people I know, working in a top Suffolk County law firm, and she knows how to use that to her advantage to weed out the crazies. She'll bat her eyelashes and show a little skin, but God forbid you try and challenge her intellect or video-gaming skills. You'll be picking up your balls from down the block. She's like Julia Roberts in *Erin Brockovich*, only with smaller teeth.

"He's just a nice guy who moved back from living in Cali for the past couple of years," she continued as I grabbed a bottle of water from the fridge.

"Nice?" I said. "That translates to 'scary troll who eats kitty litter' in my book, Nicki."

She sighed. "He's not scary, nor does he like pussy of any variety."

I almost choked on my water. I constantly forgot how my sister took after my mother, especially when it came to her trucker's mouth.

"Why the hell would he move back here after being in California, then? It's fucking Long Island!" I snapped, wiping the water off my chin.

"Umm... dodo. You moved back here too," she pointed out.

"Yeah, I moved back here from Honky-tonkville, not the land of wine country and leather skin. There's a huge difference."

"Oh, get over it," she chastised me. "You're being judgy again."

Yes, I was, because I love my sister very much but her taste in men can range from Ryan Reynolds to Russell Brand, so excuse me for being a little worried here.

"He's really cute and said that the LA lifestyle just wasn't for him," she reassured me.

"Christ." I rolled my eyes, "It's bad enough he lived in California, but now you're telling me he's an LA fag? Talk about judgy. They're the fucking *worst*! Lemme guess. His quote, unquote acting slash cater-waiter career didn't work out the way he planned?"

Silence on the other end of the phone answered my question.

"Thank you," I said.

"It was actually a reality show, but, you know, I'm just trying to help you here," she said, slightly hurt. "Ma told me you've barely gone out since you came back."

Unfortunately she was right. Besides hanging out with my mother and uncle, I had only gone out that one time with Sean. I only went to the supermarket when I needed food, which was rare because my mother cooked almost every other day for me. Mostly I just sat in front of the television watching Wendy Williams and reruns of *Supernatural*. Who needs a life when you have a sassy black lady as a gossipy best friend and two hot brothers to drool over every day? I had no interest in going out to another bar to see the same people sitting on the same barstools like they had for who knows how many years.

"I hate everyone," I responded.

"You're an asshole. Try and remember that if he texts you," she said, and I reluctantly agreed to myself that she might be slightly right. "And if he texts you, try not to be anything like you. Try and be nice. Promise?"

"Yes, sister dearest," I sweetly said. "What's Mr. La La Land's name?"

"Sebastian."

"Of course it is," I whispered. Jesus, even his name sounded like he belonged in the Valley.

"Okay, I have to go," she said before I had a chance to add anything else snarky. "Love you, and be nice to him!"

"Yeah, yeah. Can't make any promises. Love you too. Bye." I hit End on my phone.

I put the phone down and sighed deeply.

I really should have had my Xanax prescription renewed.

It was during my Friday afternoon ritual of doing laundry and cleaning my house that I heard my phone beep, indicating I had a text. I picked up the phone and saw a new message from a number I didn't recognize. I typed in my password and opened the text.

Um. Hi. Is this Robby?

I slowly rolled my eyes at the misspelling of my name and texted back.

Yes, this is RobbIE. Who might you be?

Ten seconds passed and my phone beeped again.

Sry. This is Sebastian. Ur sis gave me ur #?

Damn Nicole. I'd already corrected him once, and now he was using abbreviations like a thirteen-year-old. She was not going to make this easy for me.

Ah, yes. Sebastian. How are you today?

Im doin ok. U?

Fantastic. Just finished cleaning my toilet.

Well, I was being honest. I did smell like Pine-Sol, but Christ, I'm a retard.

Sounds fun. ;)

How cute, a winky face after I said I'd just cleaned my shitter. How was I supposed to respond to that?

Very thrilling. Can't think of anything else better to do. ;)

Okay, that was lame, but seriously, I'm talking about Scrubbing Bubbles here.

He didn't respond, which probably meant he went over to my sister's desk and backhanded her for getting him into this. Served her right for trying to set me up. The phone beeped again about ten minutes later.

Sry bout that. Someone called.

No problem. So, what's up?

Not 2 much. Wanted 2 see if you would wanna hang l8r? Maybe din or sumthin?

I looked at the phone like it was an alien object. I knew it had been a while, but had I just been asked out on a date by a horrifically spelled text, or was "din" short for something gay and sexual that had been invented since my time in Foster?

Umm.... Sure?

Kewl. :)

I fucking hate that word, if you even want to call it a word. Nicole's voice echoed in my head telling me to behave.

Yeah. "Kewl." You sure you don't want to chat on the phone first?

Nah. Its all good. I'll come by @ 7 & see how it goes.

Huh? How what goes? If I open the door and if he finds me scary, he'll just turn around and run for the hills? I know James told me to let go and "be breezy" but this was ridiculous.

I suppose so.... Do you need my address?

Nope. Nicki already gave it 2 me. ;)

I didn't know who to be more pissed at, my sister for giving a stranger the location of my bedroom where he could come kill me during the night, or the guy who'd just called my sister the nickname I called her. Whichever it was, I didn't let on and wrote back.

See you at 7 then.

Kewl ;)

This was going to be a disaster.

I'D HAD the idea of setting Tyler up by making the excuse that Riley and I were having a small dinner party. A chance for Tyler to mingle with our own kind in their natural environment. When he asked me if this was just a lame excuse for us to set him up with one of our friends, I got pissed at him and yelled, "Fine. Don't come, bitch. I'm sure we can feed another dozen people on what you would eat alone." Of course it was a lie, but I really needed him to have a life of his own, and the only thing that made Tyler do anything was fear that someone somewhere might not want his company. So telling him not to come was the quickest way to get him knocking at the door.

The night of the party, I opened the door with an evil grin on my face. "Enter freely and of your own will," I said to Tyler, moving aside and taking the bottle of wine he brought. "Oh look, wine without a screw-off cap. See, we are having an effect on you."

"Suck it," he said and started to look around at the near empty living room. "Am I that early?" he questioned.

At that moment the only other party guest walked out from the hallway, drying his hands on his pants. "Hey, you sure this guy is going to show up?" He noticed Tyler and paused.

"Okay, so it is a lame attempt to set you up with one of our friends, so get over it," I said, still standing in front of the door.

Thank Jesus Riley came out from the kitchen, because I was fairly certain Tyler was going to gut me like a fish any second.

"Hey, you made it," Riley said, as friendly as he could. "Have you met my friend Jim? He works out at my parents' ranch."

Jim was a sweet and somewhat handsome man who was a little older than the three of us. Maturity meant nothing as he looked Tyler up and down like he was fresh meat.

Tyler forced himself to smile, and he shook Jim's hand lightly. "Pleased to meet you," he said like a wooden mannequin.

Another fun night began!

"Hey there," Jim said, gripping Tyler's hand firmly. "Pleased to meet you too."

"Great, so we're all here," I said, trying to make light of the already disastrous evening and moving quickly toward the kitchen, staying clear of any fists that might be headed toward my face. "How about we pop this baby open and get the night started?" Because nothing defused a potential gay bomb of drama like a bottle of wine. Of course a little alcohol could also go a long way in making things worse, but screw it. From the death glare Tyler was shooting at me, I had literally nothing to lose. I grabbed a corkscrew and pulled the cork out of the bottle with one smooth movement. Years of practice.

"I've heard a lot about you," Jim said as he and Tyler moved toward the breakfast nook where I was pouring the wine.

"Oh really?" Tyler said, giving me an all-new deadly glare he had stowed away.

I ignored it, of course, and just smiled as I handed him a large glass of wine.

"Yeah, sometimes these two won't shut up about you," Jim said, taking his own glass.

"Oh yeah, they can be like that," Tyler said, downing half the glass in one swallow. "Always full of surprises."

"Is there a surprise coming?" Jim asked, confused.

"Count on it," Tyler replied. He literally snarled at me before finishing the glass in another gulp. "Hit me again." He slid the glass back toward me with a look that blared *before I hit you.*

"Someone likes cheap wine," I muttered under my breath as I filled his glass again.

"So Tyler runs the sporting goods store over on First Street," Riley explained in his always polite way to break the tension.

"Oh, is that fun?" Jim asked, doing a good job at faking interest.

"It pays the bills," Tyler said, trying his best not to be a complete asshole, I suppose.

There were a few seconds of uncomfortable silence before Jim offered, "I handle the steers over on the ranch."

"Oh, is that fun?" Tyler asked him, parroting Jim almost perfectly. Alert! Asshole Level One reached!

"It pays the bills," Jim countered, obviously confusing the partially buzzed Tyler.

Tyler tried to laugh, but it just came out so hollow. "I'm sorry," he half apologized. "Robbie, can I talk to you for a moment?" Suddenly he didn't sound as buzzed as he had thirty seconds before.

I stopped grating cheese and pointed to myself innocently, mouthing "Moi?"

"Yes, you," Tyler growled as he strode down the hall and away from Riley and Jim.

"Excuse us one moment, boys," I said. "Please have some fresh mozzarella while you wait." I smiled and scurried down the hall, following Tyler to the guest bedroom, where he looked like he was about to pull out all his golden locks.

"What in the hell is this?" he demanded.

"Oh no, ma'am," I warned, taking a step back from him and dropping into my bitch mode stance. "Do not come at me like I owe you money or something. You want to have a conversation? That's fine, but you best check yourself before you wreck yourself." I always hated that expression, but if Tyler was going to come all Steve Austin at me, then he was going to get a little Jaime Sommers back in his face.

He took a deep breath and looked me square in the eyes. "What exactly do you think you're doing out there?"

I arched one eyebrow. "Well, I was making sure the chicken didn't get burnt, but I have a feeling you aren't talking about my culinary skills." He was about to start yelling, but I held up a finger and calmed him down like the deranged puppy he was. "What I think I am doing is trying to get you to meet another living, breathing gay man who you can date. You know, in some cultures that might be looked on as a good thing, but leave it to Foster to fuck even that up."

"I didn't ask you to set me up."

I shrugged. "No one asks to be set up. Well, I guess some do, but those are pathetic people who aren't going to get laid anyway, so they don't count." He was about to go off again, but that didn't stop me from continuing. "Yes, we tried to set you up and yes, we lied to you because you are basically a twelve-year-old-girl when it comes to anything resembling relationships. If we told you anything in advance, you would have just run screaming into the night." He opened his mouth, but I kept going. "And yes, I know it isn't cool to just jump out with a guy you don't know, but that's the price you pay for being mentally deficient when it comes to the whole dating thing. No one is expecting you and Jim to get married! Hell, I thought he was too old for you, but Riley thought it would be easier to start you out with a pony before you tried to ride a real horse, and no, that isn't a dick joke, but it might as well be since all you know are one-night stands. So just go out there and pretend to like him for tonight. Then we can regroup and grade you on how well you did."

He opened his mouth and then closed it just as quickly, probably because the mouse in his head stopped running around in the wheel he called a brain.

"Good." I grabbed his arm and turned him back toward the living room. "So let's head out and learn to play nice with others, okay?"

The night wasn't going to go up in flames if I had anything to do with it. Even if I could smell the chicken burning.

I never saw Jim after that night. Riley said he'd asked once if Tyler asked about him and then nothing. For all I knew, he'd gone into a gay bad-date relocation program.

However, that didn't stop Riley and me from setting Tyler up again. We threw guys at him for the next two months. Some kind of worked, while others didn't. What I mean by that is I think he screwed at least two of them and never called again, which was high praise coming from the Talented Mr. Parker. At least he met people who were available and weren't guys he'd gone to high school with. He would go on his dates and report back to us, listing the pros and cons, even though most of the cons were shallow. Luckily for Tyler, since he was still in good shape and attractive, he could afford the luxury of being picky, unlike the rest of us mere mortals. Between Riley and me, we found a whole gaggle of gay men who lived around Foster, with a little help from Tom and other people I would see out at the bar. I had to give it to Tyler for putting up with the both of us and going out on a record number of dates during that time.

The truth is, yes, I did have my selfish reasons for acting like that bitch of a matchmaker on Bravo. However, I really did like seeing people happy and not alone when I knew they so desperately wanted to be with someone. You see, Tyler was the saddest guy I had ever met. There was this aura of misery about him that he probably didn't try to project but came off him like stink lines off a cartoon pig. He just didn't trust happy, so I thought maybe if I could spring happy on him, it would take. And, yes, I not-so-secretly still thought Riley would leave me any moment for Tyler. One of the very few times Riley got angry at me was one night when I told him about that fear. He said he would never do that to me because he loved me and could never be with someone like Tyler. It would be like him being with someone exactly like himself, and why would he want that? I knew Riley would never do anything to hurt me, but that bitchy voice in the back of my mind kept warning me to keep an eye on Tyler anyway.

Pay attention, because that voice is about to make a comeback.

No matter what he might have bitched about that night and the random other dates we forced him on, I knew deep inside Tyler appreciated having some friends, gay or straight, in his life who really cared about him.

Little did I know that would all change in a matter of seconds.

Chapter Three
Open Up the Gate—
Opportunity Is Not a Lengthy Visitor

"HONEY, YOU better give yourself an enema before you leave the house tonight," my uncle said as if he was telling me what kind of shirt I should wear.

"Uncle Jay!" I yelled from across the table. "I'm not having sex with anyone tonight. And eww, why would you discuss enemas with your nephew?"

"I'm just saying. It's been forever since someone's been up there. I hope you don't have any bats hibernating in your ass." He took a sip of his tea while trying to hide his satanic smile.

"Uck! Do not get me started on what is stuck in where, old man, or I'll tell them where Jimmy Hoffa is buried." I shook my head, my stomach turning the more I thought about tonight. "You nasty. You know that, right?"

"But of course I know that, my dear, sweet child. I'm 850 years old, and I'm allowed to say whatever the fuck I want just as long as I'm getting that social security check." He cackled. I rolled my eyes.

"I really question this family sometimes," I said to no one in particular. "I'm already nervous as fuck about going on this date thing. I don't need to be thinking about having sex with the first new guy I'm hanging out with since I've been home."

"Well, then do it for me, at least." He sighed. "All my old Gene Kelly movies are starting to get worn out, if you catch my drift."

I was about to start throwing up all over my kitchen table, but my mother came through the front door before I had the chance.

"Robbie, did you need me to iron anything for you...? James! I didn't see your broom, I mean, car," she joked as she gave her brother a kiss on his cheek. "I told you to park in the driveway. The assholes around here drive like they're auditioning for NASCAR."

"Rose, my love, calm your saggy tits," he soothed. "I didn't want to take your spot since you get so bitchy about those kind of things. Besides, I have insurance."

"I should hope so at your age." She flipped him off. Yes, they did that kind of thing regularly. "What the hell are you doing here anyway?"

"Your son here is having his doubts about his date tonight, and I'm trying to convince him to at least get some action, even if the dinner tastes like cat food."

I turned about ten shades of crimson, and my mother and uncle laughed like hyenas. "What the hell are you two laughing about?" I yelled at the both of them, which stopped the gigglefest for about four seconds. "You both are nuts. I'm not doing anything with anyone I just met. What kind of a slut do you think I am?"

Uncle James calmed his laughter just enough to say, "Robbie, no one is calling you a slut. If only you were a slut, then this would be easy. I'm saying there's nothing wrong with giving in to the hormones that have been locked up tighter than a frog's ass for years." He patted my hand. "Let them out to see the light of day—" He took a sip of his tea. "—or at least to break in your new bed." They both started laughing hysterically again while I slowly thought of ways to break his hip and get away with it.

My mother took one look at me and settled her hysterics to a more moderate chuckle. "Aww, honey, he's just joking with you. Aren't you, James?" He raised his eyebrows innocently, and my mother swatted him on the shoulder.

"What? The kid is still young, unlike us," he exclaimed. Her face went from jovial to Death Star in a heartbeat. This didn't faze him one bit because he kept talking, this time in a more serious tone. "Robbie, I know what you've been through. Believe me, I do." His gaze wandered and his eyes got glassy, but he quickly rubbed them dry. "You have the chance to have fun again and start over. Isn't that why you came back here?" I nodded. "I mean, besides seeing your favorite uncle more often, that is."

"You're my only uncle," I informed him point-blank.

"Touché," he responded.

"Yes, but that doesn't mean I'm still not scared to start over again," I said quietly.

My mother slowly placed her hand on mine. "It's not going to be easy, but the time to open your heart—"

"And your legs," James snickered. Arm smack, dirty look from his sister.

"The time is now. You're going to be fine." She squeezed my hand. "We all are." I might have built a cage around my heart, but my mother had built a whole goddamn dungeon and moat around hers.

She turned her head to James.

He rolled his eyes. "I swear, sometimes you're gayer than I am." He covered her hand with his. His smile was genuine, if a little weak.

"Thank you," I said to my mother, and James cleared his throat dramatically. "Yeah, you too, Aunt Sassy." He winked back in response. "Now go help my mother decorate something. I have to make this place and myself look presentable."

"All right, we'll leave you alone," my mother said, getting up from her chair. "You sure you don't need me to iron anything? I know how bad you are at seams."

I rolled my eyes, "No, Mother. I'm fine. Thank you."

"Okay," she said. "Come on, Jamesy-boy. The new Touch of Class catalog just came in the mail. This time I'm thinking the beaches of Saint-Tropez."

Uncle James dropped his head and shook it slightly. "You do know we live in *Ronkonkoma*, New York, right?" He got up out of his chair and slowly followed her to the door. He stopped and turned just before the doorframe. "Robbie?"

I stopped cleaning the table and looked over at him. "Yeah?"

"Just remember something," he said. I nodded to indicate I was ready to hear the rest of his sentence. "Opportunity is not a lengthy visitor."

I smiled at him gently. It was a quote from one of my favorite Stephen Sondheim musicals, *Into the Woods*. "I know," I replied.

"Good." He smiled and started to walk out again, but then paused. "One last thing. You sure you don't need anything else for tonight? Sex tips? Condoms? Strawberry-flavored lube?"

"Get out, you crone!" I yelled, pointing to the door.

I saw my mother's hand appear from nowhere and grab his wrist to drag him out the door.

I silently wished she would put him on time-out for the next eighty years.

I went through my closet at least eighty-five times trying to figure out what to wear on a date. A date being something I hadn't been on in roughly seven years. Not only was it a date but a fucking blind date that my sister, of all people, had set up. I felt nauseated but, as my Uncle James had so eloquently put it, it was time to start a new chapter in my life.

And I needed to get my ass laid.

He was right. Mostly about starting new, but getting laid wouldn't be a bad thing, I supposed. Sean Cody had enough of my money. That's a porn site, for all you prudes out there. You're welcome in advance.

My thoughts went into overdrive as I tried out ten different combinations of outfits and wondered how the hell I'd ever owned a clothing store. The conversation with Uncle James and my mother was something I'd really needed to have, even if I'd squirmed like a two-year-old being force-fed mashed-up peas throughout the whole thing.

Why can't people have more than one happy ending? What if the prince finds another princess or, as in my case, dies? Does

Cinderella's story end too? Does she go back to washing her stepfamily's dirty clothes? No. She'd live, and that's what I was going to do.

That's what Riley would want me to do, and he was always right.

The one thing he ever did wrong was be right.

He was a goddamn saint. I could've blown up a church and then murdered half the football team and he wouldn't have blinked an eye. As long as I knew what I did was wrong, he would've forgiven me and never spoken about it again. I, on the other hand, being a full-blooded, thick-headed Italian New Yorker, would've lost my mind, and if I didn't crack his skull with a saucepan, I would've "forgiven" him by never letting him forget what he'd done well into the ever after.

I like to hold a grudge; what can I say? You fuck up with me once, you're dead to me. That's just the way it is. Riley always saw the good in people. I wondered what color handbasket those same people were taking down to hell. I wasn't always right—and by "wasn't always" I mean "most of the time was." I thought Tyler was trying to take Riley away for the longest time, but I can safely say that was never the case. And when Riley died, we were both stubborn assholes for far too long. It took the very real threat of another tragedy for us even to start acting like human beings toward each other. Forgiveness and friendship finally won out.

Lucky for him, love was also something Tyler won with Matt. He'd found someone who was as perfectly broken as he was and from what I'd been told by Tyler since I left, they were doing well.

Now here I was, after the worst time of my life, getting ready for a date with a guy I didn't even know anything about except that his name was Sebastian and he worked in the IT department of my sister's job. Not to be too shallow here, but if he looked like *Revenge of the Nerds Part 27*, I would skin my sister alive.

I went through my mental Rolodex, trying to figure out if I remembered any Sebastians from my gay Long Island youth. I came up with about fifteen, and most of them were huge sluts from what I could recall. This guy might as well have been named John, Chris, or Mike, because every other gay man living on this island had those names.

Seriously, I'll show you a map one day.

Around six o'clock I decided on something remotely decent to wear—but secretly knew I would change my mind later—and laid it out on the bed. I went to the bathroom to start the shower but looked into the mirror just before I turned the water on.

I hated my hair. What was left of it, anyway. I was convinced that, living in Foster for so long, my once thick hair had become so traumatized that it had quietly started to retreat to the back of my skull.

Or it could be that most of my male relatives were practically bald by the time they reached thirty.

Fuck you, genetics.

I'd given up gelling the fuck out of the sides to make an optical illusion that I had more hair. If I was going to be starting over, I needed something fresh and new.

I looked through the bathroom drawers until I found the old hair buzzer I'd used to give Riley crew cuts during the hot months in Texas. I would rub his head for good luck and he would laugh because I'd tickled his scalp. I pulled the buzzer out of its plastic bag and put it up to my nose. I could still smell a faint trace of the coconut shampoo he used when he washed his hair.

It's really true what they say about certain scents bringing memories charging back like an out-of-control freight train. I quickly blinked out a drop of water that developed in my eye and plugged the clippers into the socket. I placed it on the counter while I stripped down to my underwear and laid an old towel on the floor so I wouldn't have to be chasing hairballs around the house for the next three months.

I picked up the buzzer and took a long look in the mirror at the random mop atop my head. I breathed in the scent of Riley's shampoo that I knew would be gone as soon as the machine touched my scalp.

"Well. Here goes everything," the person on the other side of the glass told me in my own voice.

I took a deep breath, turned the switch to On, and placed the buzzer to the side of my head. One stroke and my hair looked like someone had just mowed a path in two-foot-high grass. *Maybe I could start a new trend?* I laughed to myself and continued to cut, watching the clumps of hair fall to the floor. Tiny specks of gray occasionally caught my eye.

Christ, how long had I had those?

The vibration of the buzzer relaxed me, and before I knew it, I'd finished. I twisted the mirror in every direction to make sure I hadn't missed a spot. All I needed was to look like one of those monks at the airport for my date tonight.

When I knew I was done, I turned the clippers off, put it on the counter, and pulled the plug out of the wall. I looked at my reflection and cursed myself for not going all Anne Hathaway by singing "I Dreamed a Dream" while I was cutting. I had to make myself laugh because I was actually freaking out. My hair was gone. Most of it lay on the towel I was standing on and some little bits were hanging on to my nose for dear life.

I hadn't shaved down to the skin because I wanted people to know there had once resided a mane where a five o'clock hair shadow now showed.

I smiled regardless. I liked what I saw and was grateful I didn't have a cone-shaped head.

Those genetics I was happy to inherit.

As much as I would have loved to be all Mulan-y looking at my reflection, the remnants of chopped follicles were starting to itch the fuck out of me. I cleaned up the bathroom, took a quick shower and threw on some sweats to wear before rethinking my wardrobe for the rest of the night. I gathered up the hair-covered towel and went outside to shake it out into a trash can where, hopefully, raccoons wouldn't choke on it.

I was about to go inside when I looked through my mother's back window and saw my sister standing there with a coffee cup in her hand, talking to someone, who I can only imagine was my mother. Not that I wasn't happy to see her, but I wondered why she was there on a Friday night. I made my way to Mom's back door; something inside me thought this was no random visit on my sister's part.

I swung open the door and the two of them looked like I had caught them with their hands in the cookie jar. Then their gazes moved to the top of my head.

I rubbed my fuzzy scalp and rolled my eyes. "What? Too butch?"

They slowly turned their stares to each other and then looked back to me standing there, waiting for an answer.

"It's… different," my mother offered cautiously.

"You look like a plucked chicken!" Nicole squealed and fell into a laughing fit.

"Nicole Marie!" my mother shouted angrily, while I glanced around the kitchen, looking for a blunt object to throw at my sister's giggling face.

"I'm sorry," Nicole breathed as she wiped the tears out of her eyes. "But holy shit! Why'd you do that?"

I turned red and gritted my teeth. "Because I wanted to try something different. That's why."

"I think it looks nice," my mother said above Nicole's giggling. She swatted her on the arm and gave my sister a look that immediately reduced Nicole to the five-year-old Mom had caught raiding her makeup.

"Why are you here anyway, Nicole?" I asked. "It's Friday night. Shouldn't you be at a karaoke bar drunkenly singing Kelly Clarkson or something?"

She squinted at me, which roughly translated to "Fuck you."

"No, I came to visit Ma and have some coffee. That's all."

I crossed my arms and cocked a disbelieving eyebrow. "Oh really?" I said, looking back and forth between the two of them. They looked blankly at me for a moment, then focused their attention on anything but my face.

"All right," I sighed. "What the hell is going on?"

"Nothing, sweetheart," my mother said with a pitifully guilty smile. She never called me "sweetheart" unless something was up.

"Sweetheart, your goldfish, Sandy, went to go live with his friends in the ocean."

"Sweetheart, you can't dress up as Madeline Kahn in Clue. *No, not as Madeline Kahn in* Young Frankenstein *either."*

And then there was always, "Sweetheart, Daddy got into a bad car accident."

I stared down my sister. I knew I could break her if given the chance. It didn't take long.

"Oh, for fuck's sake!" she yelled. "We're both making sure that tonight goes well for you, all right? Jesus Christ." She shook her head and took a sip of coffee.

"What?" I asked, completely confused.

"Your sister and I wanted to be certain you're... okay," my mother explained with some concern in her voice.

I scratched my head and wondered if they'd been watching too many Lifetime movies about college grads getting gangbanged again.

"What do you mean if I'm... oh."

This would be the first date I'd been on since... well, since Riley. When I was living in Foster, I'd hated the town and everything within a fifty-mile radius because of what had happened. I never went on any dates or even had a one-night stand. I shut myself and my crotch off to the world.

It had taken me all these years, with the help of those I love, to let some random guy badly text me, let alone go out to dinner with him.

They looked at me with tears in their eyes, which made me well up too. As much of a pain in the ass as my sister was and as overbearing as my mother could be, they really wanted to see me happy.

I took a deep breath and wiped my eyes. "I will be fine. Thank you." I forced myself to believe those words. If I'd learned anything from James, it was how hard it is to finish one chapter in order to start a new one.

That and how fluorescent lighting was the work of the devil.

"But"—I pointed at my sister—"if this goes to shit, I'm blaming you." She looked at me with wide eyes. "I will show up at happy hour one week when you least expect it in full-on Wonder Woman drag." It was a lie, of course; Nicole knew how much I hated shaving my legs.

My mother just shook her head at us and looked up at the ceiling with her *Where did I go wrong* look on her face. Nicole and I might be adults, but we acted like bickering children any chance we got.

"Okay, I'm going back to get ready," I said as I turned for the door. I stopped just before I turned the knob and twisted my head to look at them. "And please, in the name of all things holy, do not hover in the windows when he gets here. This isn't prom."

Both their faces turned crimson because that was exactly what they were planning on doing.

I gave them both a severe glare and left the house. I took out my cell phone and checked the time. *Damn!* Quarter to seven already, which meant one of two things. If he was a decent human being, I had maybe twenty minutes to get my shit together and look halfway human, because that was when he said he was going to show up. The alternative was that I had almost an hour because he was another Long Island fag who had about as much concept of being on time as chipmunks had of the International Space Station.

That would be none at all.

The night was turning out to be on the cool side, so instead of the lighter outfit I'd chosen earlier, I threw on a plain white T-shirt and a pair of new-ish jeans that didn't feel like cardboard. I found my favorite purple plaid sweater and secretly cursed at myself for not getting all the wrinkles out. Hopefully, the restaurant wouldn't be well lit.

And then shoes. As a gay man who had owned a clothing store for three years, you might think I would have had an abundance of shoe options. You would be mistaken. The only reason I knew what was considered fashionable by the rest of the world was thanks to whatever CW show I was watching at the time.

I had three pairs of Converse, one each in red, blue, and black; one pair of dress shoes; and one pair of black work boots that made me an inch taller. I grabbed the boots and hoped the guy wasn't a munchkin. Even though I wasn't a giant, I always felt awkward around guys who were shorter than me. Also, redheads. I'm vertically and ginger-phobic.

I quickly brushed my teeth to make sure the one final cigarette I'd had that morning wasn't still on my breath. Leave it to me to decide to stop my smoking habit the *same* day I was nervous enough to projectile vomit any second.

I was about to fix my hair when I realized I had nothing to fix.

Listen, my new haircut was only an hour old; give me a break.

As I tried using the power of persuasion to smooth one last wrinkle out of my sweater, the doorbell rang and my heart jumped up into my nostrils. He was on time; that was a point in his favor.

"Coming!" I yelled and walked quickly to answer the door but stopped as my eyes focused on the picture of Riley and me on my nightstand.

"Just a sec!" I called out and snatched the frame up. I took it into the bathroom and opened a drawer, placing the picture inside with Riley's smiling face staring back up at me.

"Sorry, baby," I whispered. "Please don't hate me." I gently closed the drawer and composed myself before rushing to the front door.

I closed my eyes and took a deep breath. "Here goes nothing," I murmured and plastered a smile on my face.

I opened the door with a sweaty hand. "Hel—"

I stopped midword and forgot how to breathe. I envisioned my sister's murder in the two seconds it took for me to turn the knob and see who was in front of me. This had to be a joke she was playing on me.

He stood there with a small smile on his face because he was most likely scared that my eyes were going to pop out of my head and hit him in his ridiculously cut jawline.

He was about six inches—well, seven, technically, if I took off these damn boots—taller than me. His broad frame filled out the sports jacket he was wearing, and I highly doubted those were shoulder pads. He wore a tight-fitting black T-shirt that I could tell, even in the dusky light, clung closely to his worked-out body. He might have been wearing jeans but, since I didn't want to continue to undress him like a piece of meat, I focused my attention on his scruffy face and dark green eyes that squinted slightly when I looked into them. His face made a strange expression I couldn't read. Disappointment? Disgust? Oh, this was going to be an awesome night.

He must've noticed the change in my expression because he quickly flashed me a pearly, white-toothed smile. "Hey, I'm Sebastian." He stuck out his large hand. "You must be Rob," he said in a husky yet smooth voice that would've made my pants fall off if I wasn't wearing a belt. It was also kind of strange that he called me "Rob" instead of "Robbie."

When I pulled my body back from swooning, I shook his outstretched hand and responded with, "I most certainly hope so. Otherwise I'm wearing someone else's underwear."

If there had been a way to astral project out of my body just so I could kick myself, I would've right then.

Sebastian opened his eyes wide. "Well, we said the word underwear in the first thirty seconds of knowing each other. I think that might be a record," he said, grinning.

I had no idea how to answer that.

I was sure that smile was going to be the last expression I would see from him ever. I waited for him to turn around and zip out of there like the Roadrunner. Instead he let go of my hand and laughed softly while he scratched at his gelled crimson-brown hair.

There was something about that one little nervous tic that gave me a strange sense of déjà vu. I shook the thought out of my head. I'd seen the shy, cute guy act a gajillion times in movies.

"Won't you come in?" I asked and stepped aside to let him enter. "I just have to grab my coat."

He nodded slightly and stepped over the threshold. I closed the door behind him, which accidentally gave me the opportunity to check out his cute bubble butt.

Fuck. James was right. I really did need to get laid. I mean, there were plenty of good-looking men in Foster, but I'd never given them a second thought because they were, well, from Foster, which said it all. There was obviously only one exception to the rule.

He looked around my house, taking everything in, and I cursed internally, thinking I should've butched the place up a little more before he came over.

"Nice digs," he said as he walked around my living room.

"Oh," I said as I put on my coat. "Thanks. My mother and crazy uncle did it up for me as a surprise before I moved back."

"Who's this guy?" he asked, pointing to a black-and-white photo of a man at a piano. "He your gramps?"

"Ha! I wish!" I laughed a little too loudly. "No, no. That's Stephen Sondheim, my own personal god."

Sebastian frowned. "Never heard of him."

"Wait, seriously?" I said, disappointed.

He shook his head. "Is that a bad thing?"

"It depends on what side of Broadway you walk on," I responded.

By the look on his face, he didn't seem to understand.

"He's one of the greatest composers of musicals in all of history," I said proudly.

"Oh," Sebastian grunted. "Did he do that one about cats or something? My mom used to play that soundtrack all the time when I was younger."

I cringed. "Original Cast Recording," I corrected automatically.

"What?"

"It's called an original cast recording when it's the music from a stage show sung by the original members of the cast," I explained. "A soundtrack is from a movie and can be all types of songs. And to answer your question, no, he didn't write *Cats*. That was Andrew Lloyd Webber."

"I also know *Oklahoma!*" he threw out and saw my distaste. "Well, kinda."

I just stared at him, aghast at what gay culture was coming to these days.

"Right," he said. "So you ready or…?" Either he was really hungry or he just wanted to get this night over and done with so he could go home and regret that he'd ever met my sister.

"Yes." I gritted my teeth and grabbed my wallet and keys.

He walked out the front door, and I reviewed a mental checklist quickly to ensure I hadn't left any appliances on and that I had fresh breath.

"You coming?" he asked impatiently from my front porch.

Great, now he was pissed. "Sorry," I said as I locked the door. "Just making sure I didn't forget anything. Ready when you are!" I smiled at him.

He shot me a look I assumed to mean *I've been ready, dumbass*. I followed him to the end of the driveway where his blue Jeep with California license plates was parked. It wasn't anything fancy, and by the scuffs along the bumper, I could tell he must've driven it cross-country back to Long Island. It wasn't anything special—not like I cared. I mean, I drove a Bug, for Christ's sake.

As I got in, I glanced casually toward my mother's front window and saw two shadows duck when Sebastian put on his headlights. I rolled my eyes and made a mental note to deal with those two later when this travesty of a night was over.

Which would most likely be in an hour.

Before he pulled out of the driveway, Sebastian looked in his rearview mirror, I assumed to check for oncoming traffic.

Had he just winked at his own reflection? I guess he was checking himself out instead of the road.

He glanced at me with that same strange look as before and pursed his lips like he was thinking way too hard about what to say. Or maybe he wanted to just drop me off at the next corner.

Awkward silence filled the car as we drove to the unknown destination. I had no choice but to break it since Narcissus was too busy driving and/or wondering if he should just push me out of the car. "So where are we going to dinner?"

"Just a little Italian place," he said. "Nothing special." I could've sworn he gave me a side eye after that last part.

My bitch meter was slowly rising every second I breathed the same air as him. I promised myself to find out how much spaying Nicole would cost; it was her fault I was going through this. I took a deep breath and silently prayed to Cher for patience.

"How did LA treat you?" I asked with as much politeness as I could muster. "Too much sun and plastic for you?" Okay, maybe that last part wasn't polite as much as it was snarky.

"Something like that," he said, deadpan. "It wasn't what I was looking for." This time I know he gave me the stink eye.

I ground my teeth slowly. "What exactly were you looking for?" I asked. The car suddenly stopped.

"We're here," he announced and shut off the engine.

I was about to comment on how quick the ride was when my phone vibrated in my pocket. As if on autopilot, I pulled out the phone to see a message from Kyle. My brain finally kicked in, reminding me I was actually being kind of rude. Sebastian looked over but didn't say a word. Instead he unbuckled his seatbelt and got out of the car, closing the door loudly.

Okay, I know what you're thinking. "Couldn't you just have waited to go into the bathroom and check your phone like a normal person?"

The truth is, I am far from normal. First of all, I hadn't been on a date in forever, and honestly, I didn't even remember if texting was around back when I had last dated. Secondly, whenever my phone rang at strange—and sometimes not so strange—times of the day, my heart started racing because I thought something bad had happened.

Unfortunately too many events in my life had occurred to make me act that way.

Sebastian was already out of the car, so I quickly unlocked my phone to read the message.

Fairiest of Godmothers.... So met a nerd in class and am rehabilitating him into the world of the tasteful. See you were wrong, I am not the biggest nerd in the world, I'm just his fashion advisor.

I laughed out loud and texted *BAHAHAAHAHAHAHA!!!* back, thinking about the messy blond moptop I'd met years back who not only saw the softer side of Sears, but also changed my life for the better.

It's not funny, people say I have taste.

BAHAHAAHAHAHAHA!!!

You do know when you laugh like that you cackle like a witch?

BAHAHAAHAHAHAHA!!!

Ok fuck off.

BAHAHAAHAHAHAHA!!!

I hate you and everything you stand for.

Aww, my little cupcake… I love you and everything about you though. Lemme call you later. I'm in the middle of something. XOXO

The night was beautiful, so I wasn't surprised to see so many people hanging about. I glanced out the windshield and saw Sebastian standing outside tapping his foot as he scoped out a way through the crowd walking around the little strip-mall courtyard.

It took me a second to realize where we were. Neon lights spelled out the name Buon Appetito in red and green in a wide window across the way. The sign was still the same as it was when my mother would take Nicole and me there almost every weekend when we were younger and she didn't feel like cooking. The garlic knots dripped with butter and tasted like heaven. Even though it had been years, my stomach had never forgotten about this place. The strip mall itself had changed quite a bit over the years, with different stores and an Irish pub on the corner, but the restaurant looked like it was stuck in a time warp.

"Holy shit. I love this place!" I said out loud. "God, you should see what they call Italian food down in Tex...." I was talking to no one because Sebastian had already arrived at the front of the restaurant.

What the hell was this guy's damage? Was I so hideous he couldn't even walk with me to the mildly busy restaurant? Guess he wanted to make sure no one saw us in public together.

I walked slowly. He was looking at himself in the reflection of the glass door, fixing his already perfect mane, and he winked again.

"It's okay, Ken," I said. "I think you'll still be invited to Barbie's beach party even with a few split ends." I smiled at my little joke. Him, not so much.

I cleared my throat. "Shall we?" I opened the door.

"Yeah," he said weakly and walked in. I followed right behind him.

The place looked exactly the way I remembered it. It wasn't anything elaborate or beautiful; in fact it looked like HomeGoods had thrown up all over the walls. There were gaudy light fixtures and fake fruit hung everywhere. But the smell, dear God, the smell made my stomach growl like a rhino. The scent of tomatoes and fresh bread and basil filled my nose. I smiled at the memories of Nicole and me racing to see who could finish their spaghetti first. My mother would yell at us, fearing we would choke.

The young girl behind the hostess podium broke me out of my trance when she walked over to us, snapping her gum with every step. She didn't bother to say "Follow me" as she grabbed two menus from a shelf and placed them on a table right in front of the large window.

"Your server will be right with you," she said to us, and she turned her back before Sebastian could complain about where we were seated. At least that's what I gathered since he looked like he wanted to leave rather than sit in the open.

I took my coat off and sat down, eagerly opening the menu even though I knew it by heart. Sebastian pulled off his sports jacket, and the sight did not disappoint. I averted my eyes to the appetizers because I didn't want to get caught in mid-eyefuck. I poured myself a glass of the complimentary house wine on the table. I had no idea what kind it was; it contained alcohol, and that's all that mattered.

There were a few people scattered about the room, enjoying their meals. As much as I loved the place, the new bar at the end of the strip mall seemed to be where customers flocked.

"Ever been here before?" I asked Sebastian, who held the menu in his hands but was staring over it to where the hostess had walked off. I waved my hand in front of him. "Sebastian? You in there?"

"Huh?" he said, looking back at me. "Sorry, I thought I knew that girl from somewhere."

"Old girlfriend?" I teased.

He squinted at me. "No."

I looked back down at my menu and raised it slightly so he couldn't see my face turn red. I took a glance over at the hostess and noticed she was typing away on her phone. Must be nice to get paid to be on Facebook all night.

I peeked over the top of my menu at Sebastian, who seemed to be intensely trying to set his on fire with his *Firestarter* powers. "You want any appetizers?" I asked.

"Yeah, sure, whatever" was the response.

"Ohhhhh-kay," I said quietly as a familiar older man with gray hair and mustache came over to our table.

"*Buona sera*, boys," he said with a thick accent that I instantly remembered. "How are you tonight?" He looked up from his pad at Sebastian and nodded politely; when he turned to look at me, a wide smile broke across his face. "Roberto! Is that you?"

"Gianni." I stood up to shake the hand of the man who had served me countless meals in my youth. "It's good to see you."

He slapped my hand away and pulled me into a big Italian bear hug. "Are you crazy?" he said. "I do not shake hands of the people I call *famiglia*."

Gianni was a good man and an even better businessman. He treated his customers like they were his own family. He'd owned the restaurant for as long as I could remember. If he wasn't in the kitchen creating some new masterpiece, he was waiting tables on slow nights and striking up conversation with his loyal regulars.

"Let me look at you." He let go of me and took a step back. "Your mother was right. She told me you were getting too thin."

"Of course she did." I could only imagine the conversation my mother had with him. She'd probably told him I only ate corn and roasted roadkill during my time in Texas.

I sat down and noticed a very fidgety Sebastian. "Oh damn, sorry. Gianni, this is Sebastian. Sebastian, this is Gianni. He owns the restaurant."

"Welcome," Gianni said as they shook hands.

"Thank you, sir," Sebastian said, nodding.

"Firm handshake and polite," Gianni said and then winked at me.

Gianni might have been old school, but he'd always accepted me and my rainbow without hesitation or judgment.

"The place still looks wonderful, Gianni," I told him.

He looked around the dining room, his eyes sad. "*Grazie*, Robbie. I'm doing what I can." His eyes got a little watery but he quickly wiped them dry and smiled. He was a proud man, and it made me smile. "I'm so happy that you are back home." He squeezed my shoulder. "And I know it's been some time, but I'm so sorry to hear about what happened."

I looked down at my menu and muttered a small "Thanks." If my mother had discussed my weight, no doubt she had told Gianni about Riley.

He let go of my shoulder, and I looked up to see Sebastian staring at me curiously.

Gianni cleared his throat. "So what can I start you boys off with? Some garlic knots, perhaps? I remember how much you loved them, Roberto." He turned to Sebastian. "He and his sister would have contests to see who could eat the most in a minute. I had to make a fresh batch quickly just so I could feed the rest of my customers every night!"

Sebastian raised an eyebrow and laughed while my face flushed again. At least he was amused.

"Garlic knots sound great, Gianni. And maybe some fried mozzarella?" I asked Sebastian, who just shrugged his shoulders.

"Okay, I'll go put them in now while you two decide what you want for your entrees," Gianni said. He patted me on the back gently. "It's so good to see you." He smiled and walked back to the kitchen.

I couldn't help but smile too. "He's a good man," I said.

"He seems cool," Sebastian said as he looked up and down the menu.

"Very," I responded. "He came right off the boat and created this place from nothing. Never been married and all his family is back in Italy."

"Sounds like a pretty lonely life," Sebastian said.

I looked up at him, and there was something about his eyes that seemed empty. I knew that look. It stared back at me when I looked into the mirror sometimes. "Yeah" was all I could say.

I smelled the garlic before Gianni made his way back to the table with the basket of knots. "Here you go, my boys! Enjoy," he said as he placed them in the middle of the table. "If you're ready, I'll take your order now."

I wasn't even thinking about the main course because I was wondering if I could unhinge my jaw to devour the deliciousness in front of me.

The garlic knots, people, not the guy.

"I know what I want," Sebastian quickly said.

"Certainly, my friend." Gianni whipped out a pencil and small notepad. "What can I get for you?"

"I'll have the Chicken... Fran... Frankincense?" Sebastian failed adorably at trying to pronounce "Francese." "Please?"

I giggled, and he looked at me. "What?" he said, not understanding the joke.

"It's 'frahn-chaise,'" I said phonetically. "But A for effort."

Sebastian's cheeks turned slightly red, and I immediately regretted correcting him. Gianni stood there and said nothing, only giving me a look that said *You silly boy.*

"I'll have the same, Gianni," I said softly, and he took both of our menus.

"*Grazie*, boys," he said with a warm smile. "I'll be back soon."

I smiled and nodded as he left. Sebastian grabbed a garlic knot and started chewing on it. Was it odd that he looked ten times hotter when he did that?

I grabbed one and politely tried not to scarf it down in one bite. "Damn, that's good," I thought I said to myself. When I heard a chuckle from across the table, I knew I'd spoken out loud. "Sorry, it's just that it's been so long, and goddamn, what does he put in these things?"

Sebastian smiled. "I don't know. Maybe 'fran-chaise,'" he said with a raised eyebrow.

I swallowed the piece of bread in my mouth without fully chewing it. "Okay, I deserved that," I said. "I didn't mean for that to come off so condescending."

He shook his head. "It's fine. Nic warned me about you already. She said you might do that if I brought you here." He smirked.

"Oh, did she?" I asked. "Remind me to thank and then smack her later."

He laughed his deep laugh, which made me both relaxed and excited at the same time.

"I'm picky about my people's language," I said, gulping down some wine. Whew, was it getting hot in there?

"Your people?" He leaned in. "The Italian Grammar Nazis?"

"Shut up." I laughed and almost threw a garlic knot at him, but then thought what a waste it would've been and popped it into my mouth instead.

Sebastian laughed again and made a rubbing motion to the corner of his mouth and then pointed at me. "You got a little something."

"Shit," I said as I took my napkin and wiped the greasy cheese off my lips. "That wasn't embarrassing or anything."

"Well, now we're even," he said as he raised his glass to me and took a sip of water.

"Touché," I replied and refilled my glass before taking another sip of wine. "You're not having any?" I asked, pointing to his empty glass.

"Nah," he said. "I'm trying to cut back on alcohol consumption for a bit."

"I see," I said. "Don't want to ruin your figure?" I winked.

"Very funny," he fake laughed. "Actually it's because the last time I drank, I was in a public bathroom puking up everything I've ever eaten, if you really want to know."

I put the last knot back in the basket. "No, I didn't really need to, but thank you for your honesty. I think."

Sebastian smiled evilly, scooped up the garlic knot, and chewed it happily. Sneaky bastard.

"So what brought you back here to Long Island?" I wiped hands and mouth thoroughly, just in case.

Sebastian fidgeted in his chair. "It's kind of... complicated."

"Try me," I said.

He face flushed at the same time Gianni walked over with our dinner.

"Chicken Francese!" he announced and placed the plates in front of us. "Ah, and look at that! It looks like you boys need some more garlic knots. Let me go make a fresh batch! In the meantime, *buon appetito*!"

As much as I wanted to know about Sebastian, my stomach had other things in mind. We ate quietly, and I watched the people walk around the shopping center. I looked over and, since the windows weren't soundproof, heard the overflow crowd at the bar on the corner. I went back to my meal when a familiar, squealing voice upped its volume to a scream. "*I'll fuckiinng suuue thish plaaaace! Racist basstiiiidds!*"

Both Sebastian and I looked in the direction of the bar and saw a blond guy being escorted out the front door by two burly bouncers. I almost dropped my fork when I realized the guy was a very messy Sean.

"Fuck," both Sebastian and I said at the same time. Our heads whipped around and we stared at each other, wondering why we had identical reactions.

We turned back to watch the spectacle outside. Sean screamed, *"Fuck all you biisshes!"* and flipped off the crowd that was now laughing at him. He staggered toward the restaurant, and I was in the right frame of mind to duck under the table. But I was just slightly worried Sean might get into a car and try to drive drunk.

I watched him take out his phone and push a button. "Siri? I need a fucking cab!" Whether his phone knew how drunk he was or was just used it, Sean belched and started talking into the receiver. "Hello? Yeah, I need a goddamn cab. What? Where am I? Hold on." He spun around in a circle and stopped to look at the restaurant's sign. "I'm at Bono Appy-tit-o ressrant… Five minutes? Fiiiiiine…." He hung up the phone and turned to face the window I was sitting next to. He stared right in my direction while his eyes focused.

Yes, I tried to do what they did in *Jurassic Park* by pretending not to move so he wouldn't see me, but unfortunately it didn't work.

"Guuuurrrrllll!" Sean yelled as he pointed at me and, as quickly as his drunk legs could take him, made his way to the restaurant's door.

"Shit, shit, shit," I said and looked to Sebastian, who fidgeted like he was about to jump behind the fake ficus next to him.

Behind me, I heard the bell over the door ring as it did whenever someone walked into the restaurant. I knew it was too late to escape.

"Jesus Christ," Sebastian muttered. From the sound of his voice, he'd realized he had no way out either. I watched the hostess ask Sean if she could help him and heard Sean reply, "Nah, giiiirl, I'm here to see my friend over thurr." He pointed at my table, then turned his head in my direction. He smiled at me drunkenly and then turned his gaze to Sebastian.

I watched as Sean's eyes went from glassy to bonfire in a split second. I turned back to see Sebastian look down and shake his head.

What the hell was going on?

Like I was in the middle of a tennis court, I looked from Sebastian back to Sean, who now had a satanic grin on his face as he walked closer to us.

With the amount of alcohol in his system, the next few minutes weren't going to be pleasant.

"Well, well, well...." Sean slurred as he sashayed to the table. "What do we have here?" He slowly wagged his finger at us. "Am I interrupting a date between my two-timing boyfriend and my supposed dear friend who's just stabbed me in the back?" He swallowed a burp and swayed slightly.

Sebastian's face was turning ten shades of red while I sat there trying to comprehend the words that came out of Sean's sloppy mouth.

"Boyfriend? What do you mean 'boyfriend,' Sean?" I asked, confused.

"He doesn't mean anything," Sebastian said through clenched teeth.

Sean started laughing. "Wassamatta, Sebby baby? You don't want the new slut in your life to know your secrets?"

Bitch mode unlocked.

"Sit down, Sebastian," I said calmly before he jumped out of his seat and made more of a scene than it already was. The few customers around us were looking at our table. I turned to Sean. "I'm going to let the 'slut' comment slide since you're obviously too much of a drunken asshole right now to even understand what you just called me. However, when aren't you a drunken asshole?" I asked. "Oh, that's right. When you're a high-as-a-kite asshole."

Sean's eyes widened. "How dare you talk to me like you know my life? I only had two drinks tonight, and that's because of this one!" He pointed to a furious-looking Sebastian.

From his breath I could tell those drinks must've been Big Gulp size.

"You think you can just come back here from Alabama and steal someone's boyfriend like this?" Sean spat at me. "What did you do? Follow him into the bathroom that night at the bar and let him fuck you in the stall? Didn't they teach you any manners on the plantation?"

I placed both my hands on the corners of the table, ready to flip it Jersey-style. "First of all, you know nothing about my life when I was down in Texas, you self-absorbed turd." Sean stood there with a strange expression on his face, as if he didn't know what a turd was. I continued, "Secondly, I have no idea what the hell you're talking about. I didn't do anything in that fucking bar where, once again, you treated me like some scum on the bottom of your knock-off Aldo shoes." I smiled sweetly.

Sean's nostrils flared, because he hated if anyone insulted his "style."

"Is that so?" Sean said, almost sober. "Did you lose brain cells as well as hair when you were down in Texas?"

My left hand was now two inches away from a steak knife. Somehow I didn't think the growing audience would've minded seeing a murder. "No, I did not," I said quietly.

"Well, if memory serves me correctly," Sean started, "Sebby here went to the bathroom just before you got there and didn't come out until you mysteriously disappeared from the bar."

"I got sick," Sebastian growled. "And that's only because, as I later found out, you put something in my drink, you sick fuck."

Sean's face turned beet red at the accusation.

"Hold up," I said to Sebastian. "You were getting sick in the bathroom?" My mind flashed back to that night. "Oh my God, you were that schmuck who threw up on me!"

"Holy shit." Sebastian's face went pale. "You were that bitch? I knew I recognized you!"

"Yeah, I was that bitch whose clothes you ruined," I snarled.

"Umm, excusez-moi," Sean interjected. "Are we back to me now?" He pointed to himself. "The point is, why are you on a date with my boyfriend?"

"I'm not your fucking boyfriend, Sean," Sebastian said. "We went on one fucking date where you fucking drugged me before we went to the bar you insisted on going to so you could hang out with your so-called friends." He glanced at me.

"Oh, come on, Sebastian." Sean rolled his eyes dramatically. "You were so goddamn uptight that night that I had to do something to loosen you up." He tried to laugh, but it came out as another smell-o-vision burp. "Besides, I heard you liked that kinda stuff, since it's what you used to do back in California."

I looked at Sebastian, feeling half pity and half disgust. Before he could slash Sean's throat with his butter knife, I said calmly, "Sean, why don't you go wait outside for your taxi before you say anything else you might regret later."

"I see you learned all about Southern charm." I made two fists, and he held up one hand to stop me before I got up to swing. "Please, Robbie, let's not dirty your parasol." He smirked as Sebastian reached over and grabbed my hand.

I looked down at Sebastian's larger hand covering mine, then glared at his face.

He quickly took his hand away.

Sean watched the entire exchange. "Oh, how cute. You two are holding hands already?" he said with a pout. "Seems like I came just in the nick of time to warn you, my old friend."

"Warn me that I might contract herpes by breathing the same air as you?" I smiled at him.

"Aren't you just hilarious?" Sean purred. "No, sweetie. I'd suggest hiding your ATM card, because your date is a common gold-digging whore."

If this were a Bugs Bunny cartoon, this would be the part where my eyes flashed red. Sebastian stood up, almost knocking his chair over. I grabbed his hard forearm and tried my best to pull him back down to his seat, but none of that stopped Sean from continuing. "It seems the rumors are true, since I had nothing to offer financially to this loser."

Sebastian started breathing heavily. "Shut up, Sean."

Which, of course, he didn't. "Sebby probably heard that your family's bank account is fully stocked and jumped at the first chance he got." He looked me up and down. "You didn't think he would find anything attractive about you besides your bank portfolio, did you?" He laughed like a hyena as my eyes started to sting and I was back in high school, fawning over boys I didn't have a chance with.

I looked up at Sebastian, who didn't even bother to defend himself or look at me. I let go of his arm, and he got right up in Sean's face.

"I suggest you shut the fuck up and leave," he said, loudly enough that the whole restaurant looked at us.

"Sebastian," I said as calmly as I could muster, "sit down." I saw the people around us practically move in closer. He gave me a sideways glance. "Please," I begged with tear-filled eyes.

He gave Sean one last death stare and sat down slowly. Sean, who was about to pee his pants because he realized the danger he was in, straightened his posture.

"Sean," I said to him in a level voice, "do me a favor and get your cuntface out of here before I shove your head so far up your ass you won't have to worry about scheduling another failed attempt at liposuction."

Sean sucked in his gut and didn't say another word. Instead he wove his way to the cab that had just pulled up outside.

Everyone's stares followed him and then trained back on me.

"That's all," I said to the room, and they all went back to their dinners.

I closed my eyes and rubbed my temples to help stop the room from spinning. If I didn't calm down, I was going to have a panic attack right there.

I had no idea why I was getting so upset. It could be that I thought I'd left all this bullshit behind me years ago and that things would be different.

Nope.

Kansas still stayed the same while you were off in Oz, Dorothy, a voice in my head whispered.

I didn't know what was true and what was me reacting to the ugliness that came out of Sean's mouth.

Sebastian still hadn't said a word by the time Gianni walked back into the dining room.

I smiled at him when he stopped at our table. "Sorry, Gianni, but I'm afraid I'm not feeling well, and Sebastian has to drive me home," I said and faked a cough. "Can you please put this delicious meal on my mother's account, and I will come back this week to pay for it?"

"Ah, my poor Roberto!" Gianni said. "Do not worry about it. I will do just that. Go home and get some rest." He gave me a hug, which he would have done whether I was sick or not. "Would you like some pasta e fagioli to go?"

I shook my head, "No, thank you, Gianni. I really don't think it's possible to keep anything down right now." I shot Sebastian a dirty look and gave Gianni's shoulder a squeeze. "I will see you soon and promise to stay for a full meal." I smiled at him and handed him a twenty. "And this is for the always wonderful service." I grabbed my coat as he thanked me twice in Italian.

Sebastian cautiously got up, and we both made our way to the door. I turned back to the dining room and looked at the people who were watching us leave. "Have a pleasant night, everyone! Hope you enjoyed the show!" And I curtsied before walking out to a slack-jawed Sebastian. "Close your mouth and drive me the fuck home now."

He unlocked the doors, and I dropped into my seat. He got in and started the car without a word.

The whole ride home was silent.

"So do you want to see my savings account now, or is that a second-date thing?" I asked after we pulled into my driveway.

He shut off the car and looked at me. "What the hell are you talking about?"

"You didn't disagree with Sean when he said that you were only going on a date with me because of my supposed financial status, correct?" I asked.

Listen, clearly this night wasn't going to get any better, so I might as well be the biggest bitch I could be.

He scrunched up his face like I'd farted. "You're kidding me, right?"

"Oh, come off it," I snapped as I unbuckled my seat belt and opened the door. "Typical pretty boy moves to LA, wanting to be a star, and that doesn't happen. So what does he do? He uses his looks to get some quick money and pretty gifts from sugar daddy to sugar daddy, each mesmerized by big green eyes and not knowing any better." I slammed the car door, and it creaked. "Obviously a decent car wasn't on your Christmas list."

Whoa. Where the hell did that just come from?

"Fuck you, dude!" he bellowed, following me. "Jesus Christ!" he raged and stepped over the threshold before I could close the front door. He yanked off his sports coat and threw it on the ground behind him.

I have to admit, I was slightly excited in my pants at his forcefulness. I was also mesmerized by the veins running up and down his very lovely and thick arms. However, I broke my concentration and scanned the room to see if there were any blunt objects around I didn't mind getting blood on. You know, just in case I had to throw something at his head and run.

"Why the fuck did I bother coming back here if I had to deal with a bunch of bitchy queens again? I should've stayed in LA; at least then I could get judged by better-looking people." He made a disgusted face.

I didn't need something to throw. I was going to kill him with my bare hands. "Ha! I knew it! You are such a fucking asshole!" I shrieked. "I can't believe I even agreed to do this tonight!"

"Oh, you think this has been a real treat for me either?" he yelled back. "Looks like I need to find some new friends who actually have taste!"

If I could have shot fire out of my hands, the guy would've been a pile of ash on my living room floor. "You arrogant, fucking prick!" I spat back. "You self-centered, stuck-up toolbox! You can take the boy out of LA but apparently you can't take the plastic, high-and-mighty attitude out of the boy. Sorry I'm not one of the rich, botox-injected, pec-implanted sugar daddies you're used to!"

"You're right. You're nothing but a prissy little smartass bitch who thinks he knows everything!" he fired back.

"What? Me?" I felt like Maleficent about to turn into a dragon. "You don't know me from a fucking hole in the wall."

"Yeah, I do," he said. "No wonder you and Sean are friends. You're like fucking twins on the same cycle!"

"Sean and I are nothing alike," I said flatly. "And I would hardly call what just happened proof we were ever friends."

"I couldn't wait to move the hell off of this island so I didn't have to deal with judgmental people like you!" He started for the door.

"*Are you kidding me?*" I yelled and blocked his way. "Are you fucking kidding me? Me, judgmental? Have you looked in the mirror lately? Oh, wait. You have, because you can't go past a reflective surface without stopping and checking yourself out for at least five minutes, you egotistical schmuck."

"I had something in my contact!" he screamed.

"*Likely story!*" I irrationally shouted back and panted. "I guess it's true about living out there in LA. Your ego must've tripled in size. Maybe I should wave a couple of hundreds in your face in order to get your attention."

"You can't be serious," he said. "What are you? In high school again?"

"No, but I'm sure you and your friends always looked down on commoners like me whenever you were out in whatever trendy club the Kardashians were at last." I was seriously losing it now. "You and you perfect 'roider friends must've watched *Mean Girls* like it was some How To Act Better Than Everyone manual and thought you were Regina George with all your minions surrounding you. Trying to climb the social ladder no matter who you had to step on to get there."

It *was* like I was in high school again, or worse, it was like the first time I'd stepped into a gay bar. Judging eyes staring at me. Looks of lust from creepy old men and looks of disgust from the hottest guys in the place. Something about this guy brought all those emotions back, and I was about ready to burst.

He crossed his arms and sized me up. "So does that make you the fat gay kid? 'Cause it suits you," he said with an evil smile.

"*You fucking dick!*" I roared and catapulted a throw pillow at his overinflated head.

He ducked and grabbed the pillow. "You throw like a girl!" He launched it back at me.

Since I have the reflexes of a turtle, the pillow hit me right square in the chest, knocking the wind out of me and throwing me back onto my couch with a thud. I guess those biceps of his weren't just for show. Dazed, I looked up at him and his cocky expression quickly turned into a face of sheer terror. He ran over to me in two strides and stood in front of me with his crotch at my eye level. "Shit, Rob, you okay?" He actually sounded sincere. "I... I don't know my own strength sometimes."

I looked up into his eyes, smiled softly, and punched him right in the balls.

He went down like a ton of bricks.

"Yeah," I said between deep breaths, "me neither."

I sat there trying to even out my dislocated lungs as Sebastian rocked on the floor and tried to swallow his testicles back down to the lower half of his body.

"Biiiitch," he strained to say.

"Dick," I breathed back.

I slowly got up and looked down at him. "Don't think you'll forget that one now, will ya?" If I had a weave, this would be the part where I would flip it. I started to waddle away, but my foot was promptly stopped by a vise gripping my ankle. I looked down at Sebastian, who was on his knees.

I guess his nuts had found their proper home.

"And you won't forget this," Sebastian said as he twisted my foot ever so slightly, and I fell onto the couch. Again. Thank God it was overstuffed and I didn't whack my head on the end table.

He got up very carefully with a look in his eyes that made me think my minutes were numbered. I tried to sit up, but whatever air was left in my lungs had dissipated when I had fallen back on the couch.

Well, this was turning out to be an absolutely wonderful date, wasn't it? I didn't even get a free meal!

Sebastian waddled to the couch and towered over me. He leaned down until he was an inch from my face. "That was completely uncalled for," he whispered.

"You deserved it," I said back as I tried to remember if there were any sharp objects nearby.

He glared at me, and his hot breath warmed my face. He raised his right hand and grabbed the back of my neck. Great, he was going to break my spine. Awesome.

"Yes," he said quietly, "and you deserve this."

I would've screamed bloody murder, but it was impossible because his mouth was covering mine and devouring my lips.

I did what any normal person would do in that situation and grabbed his shoulders to pull him on top of me. Which, maybe, wasn't such a good idea because he had at least a hundred pounds on me, and I was already out of breath.

I didn't care, though. Do you know how long it had been since I'd had a man on top of me who didn't weigh as much as my laptop?

Oh, shut up, you watch porn too.

I ran my fingers through his shaggy hair as he kissed me deeper. I had thought my tongue was talented. Boy, was I wrong. I rubbed my hands over his back, feeling the muscles move underneath his shirt as he ground himself against my pelvis.

I felt something else I hadn't used in a while.

As he kissed me, he massaged my neck, making me dizzier than I already was. When the need to breathe became critical, we slowed down and broke apart gently to refill our depleted lungs.

He looked down at me with a shit-eating grin, and I rolled my eyes. "You're still a dick. You know that, right?" I asked.

He sighed and laughed. "And you're still a bitch."

"Damn proud of it," I said, pulling him back to my hungry mouth.

Chapter Four
Both a Little Scared,
the Gleam in Your Eyes Is So Familiar

I'M NOT sure when I passed out, but I woke up around one in the morning practically falling out of my bed because I'd forgotten I was in the middle of an adult sleepover and there was a naked man snoring quietly next to me.

"What did I do?" and "Who the fuck cares?" ping-ponged back and forth in my brain for a minute or two as I shivered from not having any pants on. My T-shirt, which I hadn't taken off apparently, was giving me armpit wedgies. I pulled the fabric out from under my arms and grabbed a pair of shorts from my nightstand drawer. I looked back and watched Sebastian sleeping, and a whole slew of wicked thoughts went racing through my mind and then went racing through my....

You know what? I am not going to go into detail since I don't fuck and tell, but I will let you know that all those built-up hormones exploded everywhere a couple of hours ago.

No, that wasn't a euphemism, you dirty tramp.

Okay, maybe it was a little bit. Shut up.

Anycrap, I looked at the time again and subtracted three hours. I don't know why I thought of it just then, but I remembered texting Kyle that I was going to call him back. It was only ten something where he was, and those kids were probably up doing some gymnastic routine of their own for all I knew.

I took a chance regardless and tapped Kyle's name on my phone as I made my way outside to not wake Sebastian up.

Also, I reeeeally needed a cigarette.

The phone rang three times before Kyle answered with a melancholic "Hey."

"What's wrong?" I said, knowing the kid too well.

"Why does something have to be wrong?" he whined as I lit up.

"You want to go three rounds about why I am asking what's wrong or d'you want to just come out and tell me?"

Kyle exhaled his patented long-suffering sigh and told me the story about Brad getting a job at the local gay gym—of course he did—and magically moving up the corporate ladder in a matter of hours. From what I heard, Kyle threw a hissy fit, and Brad walked out of their apartment.

"Oh," I said when he got to the end.

"Oh?" he asked. "Just oh?"

"Well, I don't know if you're in a place to hear what comes after the 'oh.'"

"How am I wrong?" he asked, anger creeping into his voice. "You know the guy who owns the gym is just cruising him."

"Yeah, but that's not what you're upset about," I countered.

"Yes, I am."

"No, it's not."

"Well, then, oh wise one, tell me why I'm actually upset."

"Okay, oh whining brat of little patience," I replied. "You are upset because you're threatened by the fact other people find your boy attractive. You imagine him at a gym with strangers hitting on him and you can't do a thing about it." I said all this completely trying to ignore that fact I'd gone through the exact same thing with Riley.

He said nothing in response.

"See, in Foster you were safe. There were no other gay guys except Tyler, and God knows he doesn't like his chicken still in the egg. Now you're out in the big, bad world and you think Brad is going to realize he's dating an overbearing control freak who thinks too much and he's going to leave you."

I took a long drag.

"Now here's the good news. Moose isn't that stupid—he knew you were an overbearing control freak and against all odds he loves you for it. This has so little to do with Brad and so much to do with you. I should know because I did the same thing."

"You did?" he asked softly.

"Fuck yeah." I laughed. "When we got to Foster, I spent the first few weeks there just waiting for Riley to dump me."

"Why?"

"Why?" I scoffed. "Look, you might not be aware of it, but a lot of the guys in Foster are ridiculously hot. No, not all of them, but when people like me stand next to people like Tyler, people like me tend to get forgotten. I got paranoid about that."

"What did you do?" He sounded very curious.

"Riley got fed up and called me on it. He told me that if he'd wanted to date Tyler or someone like him, then he would have, but he didn't. He fell in love with me, and I needed to accept that fact because it wasn't other guys who were going to cause us to break up. My issues would."

I looked in the window toward the motionless shape in my bed.

"But I'm right about the gym," he pointed out weakly.

"Look, Pinocchio, you have a choice. You can be happy or you can be right, but in this case you can't be both. So what if the guys at the gym drool over Brad? You've seen him naked; they haven't. You're going to have to trust that he loves you as much as you love him and let the rest of the drama go."

"Easier said than done," he muttered.

"Easier said with a couple of glasses of wine." I thought about the night I'd just had and sighed. "Look, Kyle, being with someone isn't about being right all the time. It isn't talking about every single little thing the other person does that bugs you, and it isn't about keeping score. Brad does things that bug you. You do things that bug Brad. What you need to ask yourself is if you love him enough to put up with that aggravation. If you have to think about the answer, then you're in a relationship with the wrong guy."

"What if he leaves me?" he asked, his voice cracking.

"Do you think Brad would ever leave you?"

There wasn't an answer except for some heavy breathing.

"Then get off the phone with me and go get your man back," I ordered. "You cannot leave a boy that hot and that clueless to wander around a big city for long. Someone will come by and offer him candy or something, and then you're fucked."

"Are you okay?" he asked after a beat.

I would've loved to tell a recent high school graduate about the mess I had gotten myself into, but instead I screamed "Go!" and hung up the phone.

I put out the half a cigarette I hadn't smoked and threw it in the garbage can. I swore that was the *last* one.

"Those kids will be fine. I know they will," I said to myself as I quietly walked back into the house. I crept back into bed, hoping the cool air had gotten rid of any lingering smoke smell.

I turned on my side with my back facing Sebastian. I felt a little movement from behind me as I closed my eyes. The next thing I felt was his arm wrapping around me and pulling me close to his bare chest.

I smiled and fell right back to sleep.

The sound of keys jangling in the lock on my front door woke me up.

"What the fuck?" I said out loud. Sebastian stirred but didn't waken.

From my bedroom I could see the front door perfectly. It opened and my mother and uncle stood just outside. One of them was holding a golf club and the other a salami.

I'll let you guess who held what.

"What are you doing?" I said too loudly, and Sebastian popped his messy-haired head up.

"What's going on?" he asked, his eyes semiclosed.

"Nothing," I said. "Go back to sleep."

Both of them looked at the shirtless sexpot sleeping next to me and silently screamed, making me blush.

"*Go away!*" I mouthed at them.

They smiled like idiots, and my mother gave me the international OK sign while my Uncle James used a slightly cruder gesture and winked.

I waved them away, and they closed the door behind them.

I can only imagine what they went on to talk about over their morning coffee.

I looked down to see Sebastian's hair was matted down on the left side of his face by the pillow, while the other side was going in twenty different directions. I smiled and, as if he heard me, his eyes slowly started to open.

"Good morning," I said.

He smiled with the one side of his face that wasn't mushed against the pillow. "Good morning to you, good sir," he responded in a really bad British accent.

"Jackass," I teased and poked him in his rock-hard shoulder.

He laughed. "I'm ticklish there, so fair warning."

I laughed along, then quivered a bit thinking about those shoulders from the night before.

"You hungry?" he asked, searching for his boxers on the floor.

I grabbed them from my side of the bed and flung them at his head. "You just woke up. How can you be thinking about food already?"

"I'm a growing boy! I need sustenance to keep this looking good." He winked and hypercrunched his abs as he put on his underwear.

"You're such an egomaniac," I said.

"Yeah," he agreed. "But you like it." He grinned and kissed me quickly on the lips.

"Blah blah blah" was all I could come up with as a response, since Sebastian was right.

"Hey, you got any contact solution?" he asked. "My eyes are dry as fuck."

"Yes," I said. "In the bathroom. Top left-hand drawer. Should be in there somewhere."

He popped out of bed like a two-year-old on Christmas morning. "I shall be right back, then." He walked slowly, taking a few steps to look back at me since he knew I was staring at his butt. He winked and stuck his tongue out at me before he went into the bathroom.

"You wanna eat here or go someplace?" I asked loud enough for him to hear. "I think Maureen's Kitchen is open."

"Sounds good to me," Sebastian called back over the noise of him rummaging through the drawer.

"Maureen's does have stuffed french toast." My stomach started to rumble. "You ever have that?"

I didn't hear a response, so I walked to the bathroom. "Did you ever have...."

My voice trailed off, and I saw Sebastian standing in the middle of the room holding on to a photo frame.

"Oh shit," I said, remembering that I'd put the picture of Riley and me in the drawer the night before.

He looked at me and back at the picture. "Who's this?" he asked with a little hurt in his voice. "No, wait. Let me guess. Your ex that you're still in love with?"

"It's complicated," I evaded.

"Of course it is," he snapped. He put the frame down and pushed by me to get to the living room. "Look, I know that we jumped into bed after a fucking retarded night of crazy, but I really don't want to be used as a distraction for you until you can get over what you have to get over with that guy." He turned over cushions, looking for various clothing.

"You're not a distraction," I said solemnly.

"Yeah, I've heard that before. Trust me, Robbie, I'm not as stupid as people think I am." He paused to find his other sock. "I mean, I'm not Einstein or that guy on *Big Bang Theory*, but I'm not so stupid as to believe someone keeps a picture in his drawer and doesn't have feelings still for him. So you tell me how I'm not right?"

"Because he's dead, Sebastian."

He stopped putting on his clothes and looked at me as if I was about to say "Just kidding!" When he realized I wasn't joking, he slumped on the chair.

"Rob, I'm sorry. I didn't mean to...." He looked really upset.

"Hey," I said, walking over to him, "you didn't know." I sat down next to him, and he put his arm around me. "Riley was a very special part of my heart."

"Yeah, but still, though?" he asked cautiously.

I sighed. "Yes, but in a different way."

He didn't seem convinced.

"As I said, it's complicated." I rubbed his back.

"What happened?" he asked. "I mean, you don't have to tell me. Shit. That wasn't meant to make you upset. Fuck. I'll shut up."

I dropped my hand from his back. "It's okay. I don't get upset anymore."

He looked at me with big, caring eyes. "You don't have to say anything. I understand."

"No," I said. "I think it's about time people heard my side of the story."

Don't you?

WE PULLED up to the Bear's Den and had to park across the street because some of the parking lot was flooded. Tom's drains suffered from serious Tourette's during the rainy months and turned most of the blacktop into a lake. I saw Tyler sitting in his car in one of the only dry spots, next to the building like he had that first night we met. Who knows how long he'd been waiting, but he refused to go into the place without us being the first line of attack.

I shook my head at him as he got out of the car. "Oh look, it's Foster's very own Goldilocks," I said to him teasingly. "Oh no, that boy is too old, that boy is too gay, oh when will I ever find one who's just right?" I put a hand on my forehead as I struck a damsel-in-distress pose.

"You do know I can kick your ass, like, fifteen different ways, right?" he said, grinning.

"Oh, bitch, please. You think you're so tough? Try surviving clearance day at Valentina's when she marks down the good wigs. You got nothing on New York drag queens." I snapped twice at him, shutting his shit down, to my enjoyment, and walked into the bar.

Just because Tyler was built like a brick didn't mean he could survive my acid tongue, even if he had the strength to rip out my vocal chords.

The boys followed me into the bar, and we claimed our usual spots to survey the lay of the land. Not many people were there, because the weatherman had predicted a storm coming through later that night.

"The usual, please, Scott," Tyler asked the bartender. "It's going to get bad out there tonight. I'm glad I just got new tires. The roads are gonna be solid ice once the cold air and that rain mix it up."

"Great," I said into my martini glass. "Can't wait to go home in that shit. Good thing you drive that Mack truck you call a car, babes." I elbowed Riley.

"Just be careful when you leave," Tyler warned as he paid Scott for the beer. "There's usually some asshole kids driving like it's nothing out there."

"Thanks for the concern, pookie," I teased.

"Where's Tom?" Tyler asked when he didn't notice the 300-pound man walking around.

"He's probably upstairs downing some Benadryl," I said. "This weather fucks his allergies up."

"Oh," Tyler said. "Guess it's just us young'uns, then," and he raised his beer for a toast.

The three of us clinked our respective drinks and chatted for the rest of the night. Mostly Riley and Tyler talked about the Broncos or the Flamingos or some other type of animal. I didn't know which team was what, but I knew how to sit and enjoy the view. Red-nosed and clutching a box of tissues, Tom eventually came downstairs to join our little party.

We hung out after last call. Tom would turn on the bar lights and most of the guys would scurry away like cockroaches caught in the kitchen in the middle of the night. It wasn't the first time we had closed the place down; helping Tom pick up around the tables was a pretty normal thing we did as we tried to sober up enough to drive.

"The boy with the blue shirt was cute," I casually recalled as Tyler grabbed a couple of empty beer bottles off a table.

"If he's so cute, you date him," he threw back.

"Hey!" Riley protested. "He wasn't cuter than me, right?"

I gave him an *Aww, puppy!* look and moved over to kiss him on the cheek. "No one is cuter than you, sweetheart." Riley nodded and went back to cleaning. I turned my laser-beam attention back on Tyler. "And there was nothing wrong with him and you know it."

"I honestly didn't even notice him," he lied, knowing if he said that blue-shirt guy was nowhere near his type, I would've called him a shallow prick for the umpteenth time. "Next time point him out."

I shot him a dirty look, letting him win this battle. "What else you want us to get, Tom?" I asked, dumping another load of empties into the trash.

"How about out of here?" Tom suggested. "I can pick all this up later this morning, you know."

"My mom always taught me to pick up after myself," I said proudly. "Besides I've worked enough bars to know that this is too much for one guy."

"Riley, you want to control your man?" Tom complained.

"Well, there's no evidence that I've been able to up to this point, but I can try." Riley replied, ducking quickly to avoid my swing. He lunged toward me, picked me up off the ground, and put me over his shoulder. "Will this work?" he asked, laughing.

Tom pointed at the door. "Begone and never darken my door again."

"Riley, put me down!" I shrieked, pounding on Riley's back. As much as swinging back and forth like Jane on Tarzan's shoulders was making me sick to my stomach, I secretly liked when Riley was all aggressive like that.

Oh, shut up. You'd like it too.

"Okay, I am outs," Tyler said, putting on his jacket. "Riley, where're we watching the game this weekend?"

Riley paused his rocking. "Who's playing?"

"It's A&M against Arkansas and Texas at Baylor," Tyler answered from the doorway.

"You can come over if you want. This one won't be up till after noon," he said, bouncing me once. Oh God, I felt the chunks making their way up my esophagus.

"Sounds good. I'll bring a case of Shiner," Tyler said as he walked out into the rain.

"Okay, show's over, big boy," I grumbled at Riley, reaching down to pinch his ass. "Put me down!"

Tom stood there looking and laughing at the pair of us while Riley set me down.

"You're gonna pay for that, you know." I poked Riley in the nose lovingly.

"Oh yeah?" he said seductively.

"Yeah!" I responded by poking him again, but this time in his hard tummy.

"That's it," he laughed. "You're going down, DeCaro!"

I quickly grabbed my jacket and headed for the door, "If you're lucky!" I winked and ran out with Riley close on my tail.

"Y'all be careful, y'hear," I heard Tom bellow before the door shut.

If we laughed any more, I was going to pass out, so I caught my breath for a second before I ran across the street.

After speed-walking around the clustered streets of New York City for so many years, I'd learned how to move quickly crossing a street, avoiding as many obstacles as possible, including stupid moms with baby carriages and huge puddles. Riley came from a different world where people smiled and waved to you as you crossed the street. It wouldn't have mattered, because there wasn't anything for him to avoid since there were no headlights in the road.

When I heard the car come screeching down the block, I turned quickly to make sure he was right behind me.

He wasn't.

In the distance I could've sworn I saw a mirage of Tyler still across the street warming up his car, but the only thing I focused on was the sound of rubber spinning on pavement. The car barreled down the road and hit Riley right in the middle of his body, making him tumble up over its hood. Someone screamed out of the passenger window, *"Fucking faggots!"* The car was gone in less than a second, lights still off.

I stopped breathing. Every light went out around me and my body temperature dropped twenty degrees. On their own, my legs forced me to run over to Riley, who looked like a lump of red mush in the middle of the black road.

I screamed out *"No!"* and my vision clouded as tears blanketed my eyes. "Riley! Riley, stay with me! It's okay!" I babbled. I cradled his broken body in my arms. His head bled all over my arm, but that was okay, because head wounds bleed like crazy. Anyone who'd watched *ER* knew that. And just because his breathing was strained, that wasn't out of the ordinary because he was just stunned. Anyone who watched *Grey's Anatomy* knew that. "You're okay. You're okay. You're okay. *Someone help!*" I screamed, knowing the first hour after an accident was the most important, so I needed to get him into an ambulance right away. Anyone who watched *Scrubs* knew that. I screamed again into the air, not knowing if anyone could hear me over the torrential rain. "Somebody… please…," I strained, all the air in my lungs gone. This couldn't be happening like this, this was all wrong. I didn't know how to breathe…. This wasn't how our story ended, there was no way. I couldn't remember how to breathe….

Whether Tom heard the car tires or my screaming, I will never know, but he ran outside and then shot back inside.

Riley's eyes were rolling back and forth in his skull, and he tried to move his head.

"No, baby," I said to him through my crying. "Don't move."

The ambulance would come and I would ride in the back and they'd tell me that it didn't look good and I'd pace the waiting room forever and sooner or later the doctor would come out and tell me it was touch and go for a while but he looks like he is out of the woods. And I would go into the hospital room and he'd be all bandaged up and I'd let out a sob of relief but he would be okay. He had to be. This was not how our story ended.

He started to cough up blood, turning my blue sweater a deep shade of purple. I tried to wipe whatever I could off his face with my sleeve. "Oh God, Riley, stay with me," I said as I held him closer. "Please don't leave me."

I held him as tight as I could without breaking him any more than he already was. I looked around to see if anyone else was there to help when I heard another car rev up its engine from across the street and I panicked, thinking it was the car coming back for another pass. But it wasn't: it was much worse than the fucks who had just hit Riley.

Much, much worse.

It hadn't been an illusion. Tyler had been there the whole time.

I watched as he flew out of the lot, but not before I widened my eyes long enough to look right into his.

He pulled off as if he'd seen someone mow down a squirrel and not his best friend.

My mind went through every emotion it could, and I almost forgot I had Riley's barely living body still in my arms. His breathing became labored as he took quick and shallow gulps of air.

"Shh," I whispered, "it'll be okay." I tried to get my phone out of my pocket, but I was too scared to let go of him.

He coughed again and more blood came out of his nostrils. His mouth was moving in slow motion, as if he was trying to say something to me.

"No, Riley, baby," I said in a strained voice, "don't talk."

His mouth moved again, but this time a tiny sound did come out.

"I'm sorry."

"What?" I asked as my tear ducts overflowed. "Why are you sorry? You didn't do anything wrong. Riley, I love you! Please, please, please don't leave me!"

The corner of his mouth tried to make a smile as he let out one last breath.

Chapter Five
For the First Time in Forever, Neither One Prepared

"FUCK" WAS all Sebastian said as he sat, still partially dressed, on the couch. He had barely blinked while I told the story.

"Fuck indeed," I said. "I bet my sister didn't tell you all that before she gave you my number, now did she?"

He slowly shook his head.

"Didn't think so," I looked down at my red hands. I tended to knead them like dough whenever I got nervous. Or I had to tell the person I'd just slept with about my dead boyfriend.

"I just...," Sebastian started. "I mean, did you kill that guy? That Tyler person. I mean, I totally would've lost my shit if I ever saw him again."

"No, I didn't kill him," I sighed, "and up until a few months ago, he avoided me like herpes."

"Oh," Sebastian said as looked around and scratched the little hair patch in the middle of his chest.

"You want to know what happened a couple of months ago, don't you?" I asked him.

Sebastian shrugged and stuck out his bottom lip nonchalantly. "If you wanna tell me...."

I squinted at him. "Do you always enjoy story time after you fucked someone the night before?"

He held back a laugh, and I just rolled my eyes.

"Usually the story is why I have to go and that this was fun and all but they have an early meeting and they'll call and you know." He took a deep breath. "Rob, I want to know."

I looked down at his hand on my knee and up into his puppy-dog eyes. I tried to find something insincere in those puddles of green and gold but came up with nothing. I have a finely honed bullshit detector, and either he was serious or it was busted.

"Okay, fine." I got up, and he withdrew his hand. I went to the fridge for a bottle of water and took a sip. "I'll give you the CliffsNotes version of everything up until the day I hauled ass out of that goddamn rerun of *Green Acres*."

He looked confused at my sixties television reference.

This one is going to be work, I thought as I sat back down on the chair.

Sebastian hitched a little closer, and I was temporarily distracted by the sight of his happy trail but snapped out of it when he cleared his throat.

"You were saying?" He cocked an eyebrow as he covered up his abs.

He'd pay for that.

"So," I said, taking another sip of water. "Where should I start?"

"Why don't you start at the very beginning," he said. "It's a very good place to start."

It was my turn to look confused. "Did you just quote *The Sound of Music*?"

"Yeah, so?" He looked insulted. "You think you're the only one who can make useless pop culture references?"

"No, it's just…," I stammered.

"Oh, let me guess." His expression turned into a sourpuss. "Because I'm just a pretty boy, I don't like culture? Because I was in LA, if it isn't hip and new, I didn't have time for it? Come on, Rob, tell me what else is out of my SAT score?"

"I didn't mean…." I reached over to him.

"You meant it, all right," he said, crossing his arms and turning his head from me.

"Sebastian, all I was saying was...," I pleaded, thinking I'd screwed this—whatever "this" was—up before it even began until I saw the corners of his mouth start to quiver.

I pulled my hand back. "You're fucking with me, aren't you?"

"Yuuup," he said without missing a beat or changing his expression. "And that is what we call... acting!"

"Son of a bitch." I grabbed a pillow from the floor and was about to hurl it at him when he held up a hand to stop me.

"Uh-uh." He wagged his finger at me. "You know, throwing pillows is a sign of foreplay to my kind." He grinned.

I put the pillow down and shifted uncomfortably in my chair, since my tailbone was still a little sore.

"My parents dragged my brother and me out to see the sing-along version of that fucking movie every year for the majority of my childhood," Sebastian confessed. "You would think that both of us would've turned out gay."

I shook my head. "I don't know whether to be turned on or get violently ill at the thought of you singing 'Edelweiss.'" Horror filled my expression.

He flipped me off, and I laughed.

"As you were saying...." He motioned for me to continue.

"Right." I cleared my throat, since I was about to talk about some of the worst times in my life. "Riley died."

Any humor in the room flew out the window. Sebastian's back stiffened and his mouth turned into a straight line.

I took a deep breath. Here it came....

"My mother and sister took the first flight down to Texas that they could get. I honestly don't even remember how they found out about everything, come to think of it. Riley came from a successful oil family down in Foster. Everyone knew who they were, but the Mathisons kept their private lives away from the rest of the town. I mean really hid it away. I'm sure Riley's mother kept a press staff on hand at all times just in case. They didn't want news to spread that their only son was mowed down in front of a gay bar and died in the arms of his Yankee boyfriend."

I took another sip of water while Sebastian patiently waited for me to continue.

"I sat in the back of the funeral home with my mother and sister, spaced-out in my own little world thanks to the power of Xanax. Tom was the only person I clearly remember showing up to offer his condolences. From what he told me months later, some regulars from his bar, whom I barely knew, shook my hand or hugged me. Any other so-called 'friends' with blond hair and a vast knowledge of sporting goods were nowhere in sight.

"After the burial, which I had no say in, Tom told me to come to the bar for a memorial drink in honor of Riley. I thanked him but told him I was too tired.

"It wasn't a lie.

"I was mentally, physically, and emotionally drained, and I couldn't even think about stepping back through the doors of the last place where Riley had been alive and breathing and himself, not broken. The place where we had so much fun and so many memories. Going there would've sent me over the edge I was already hanging on to by my fingertips. Worse, all I could imagine was the two pictures of him in there now. The one where he was young, smiling, and shocked to have his picture taken, and the other that was his obituary. I thought I had hated that wall before—now I loathed it with all the pieces of my shattered heart.

"For the next couple of days, I took my prescribed pill every night before I went to bed, but it never stopped the nightmares of Riley flying through the air and slamming down on the pavement like a rag doll. In every dream, Tyler lurked somewhere in the shadows, standing there staring at me with Riley's dead body in my arms. Tyler would laugh maniacally, then fade away like a spirit into the darkness no matter how many times I called for his help. I would wake up in our cold bed with a sore throat and wet cheeks.

"My mother, who was still staying with me, would run into my bedroom like I was five and scared of the bogeyman.

"However, now, the bogeyman had a name.

"I hated Tyler. I hated him for not doing anything that night. I hated him for not showing up at Riley's funeral to at least pay his respects because he was too chickenshit. I hated him for pretending he was my best friend for months, only to leave me when I needed a best friend more than ever. I hated him for haunting my subconscious while I slept." Worse and unsaid was that the more I hated Tyler, the more I hated Foster. It was as if the man was the embodiment of the town that had killed Riley, together linked in hatred and death.

I looked up to see Sebastian's fists clenched and his jaw locked. "I would've beaten the shit out of him," he said. "And then I would've left him in the middle of nowhere so he would have to find his way back to the closet he belonged in."

I saw tears well up in Sebastian's eyes, but they never fell.

"And it would've solved nothing," I said.

"I just don't know how you could've stayed down there and not wanted to scream from the rooftops about what really happened," he said. "You're a much braver and more forgiving person than me." He looked down at his hands.

"No, I'm not," I said. "I hated that place, but there was no way I was going to run off in the middle of the night to escape it. No, I wanted that town to pay, even though none of them knew the whole story. They thought Riley was just another hit-and-run victim, while I was still the little fag who worked in the shop around the corner. I made them uncomfortable with my New York accent and fashion sense. You may call that bravery, but I call it rage.

"I was angry at the town for being so clueless. I was angry at Tyler for not standing by me. I was angry because Riley left me to fend for myself in a world I knew nothing about and where I had no one close to talk to.

"The only thing that gave me some consolation was that Riley's family didn't contest the life-insurance money Riley had put in my name when he first started to work for the oil company. I'd always hated that insurance because I thought of it as a jinx.

Riley told me it was some policy that all employees were required to have whether they dug a hole or cleaned the toilets in the main office building.

"I was grateful to have the money, I guess. But the cost was too high."

"After about two weeks of being in a medicated fog, I went back to work at the thrift store old Magda ran. She was happy to see me, but also sad because she had to tell me that she wanted to retire and move to Florida to be closer to her kids.

"On one hand I understood why she wanted to leave. She was 850 years old, and the store wasn't exactly Neiman Marcus. On the other I was upset that one last thing to keep me sane in Foster was going to, literally, close up shop.

"My mind was spinning when I remembered the insurance money.

"I knew Magda's books like the back of my hand, and I had slowly coerced her into updating her point-of-sale machine, so I knew how the inner workings of the business functioned better than she did. Magda rarely had enough patience to use her flip phone, let alone a new computer system. I did most of the ordering while she sat back and did her crossword puzzles behind the counter.

"I told her that Twice Upon a Time wasn't going anywhere and neither was I. She almost broke a hip, she was so happy that her little store was going to live on even if she was thousands of miles away.

"She didn't leave for almost two weeks after I bought her out, because she wanted to make sure all her vendors knew I was taking over. Little did she know that I talked extensively with the majority of them, since I fixed any mix-ups that her ancient eyes may have not seen. I didn't want to break her heart, so I let her be."

"Your very own store, huh?" Sebastian said. "That must've been interesting, being your own boss."

"Please," I said. "I was my own boss, employee, stock boy, and cashier. It was miles away from interesting. Owning my own business in a town I hated wasn't on the list of things I wanted to accomplish in my life. The fact that town's good citizens couldn't tell the difference between Armani and OshKosh didn't make anything better…. However, a few people in Foster had some sort of fashion sense and personalities to go with it. They were far and few between but surprisingly loyal, even if their average age was about sixteen and exclusively female. I didn't really complain because I think inside every gay man, there's a teenage girl waiting to be unleashed so she can gab about the latest episode of some trashy reality show or how dumb boys are." I sighed. "At least that's what I told myself before I put on my act every day."

"What do you mean?" Sebastian asked.

I sighed again. "I was the token gay character on the CW's *Tales from Foster*. The shop became my stage and I put on a Tony-award-winning performance every chance I got. I wasn't the butchest fag on the block to begin with, but when I had a new audience to impress, I turned it up three degrees gayer."

"Why would you want to do that?" He scratched his head.

"Because if the town was going to think of me as the gay one, then that would be what they got," I confessed. "So they got the gayest version I could muster, because I knew it would make people feel even more uncomfortable that I still lived there when there really was no reason for me to."

Sebastian shook his head. "I just don't understand. I mean, you hated everything and everyone there, supposedly, and practically none of them knew about your relationship with Riley, right? Why wouldn't you just am-scray out of there?"

I let the pig Latin slide. "Somehow I didn't think my time in Foster was done. And it wasn't, but not for the reasons I thought."

"How do you figure?" He leaned closer.

"Are you writing a book on fucked-up hookups or something, Dr. Phil?" I asked.

He leaned back on the couch with a grunt. "No, I just want to know about you. That's all. Jesus."

I looked at him and tilted my head.

"What?" he asked.

"Nothing," I said and took another sip of water.

"Bullshit," he responded.

"What? What bullshit?" I almost choked on my water.

He moved closer and stared me straight in the eyes. "You're scared."

I didn't move or respond, because he was right. How he knew astonished me.

"You're terrified of letting anyone back in." He poked me right in the chest. "You've built a wall up, dug a moat, and hired an army to be on watch at all times to make sure you don't get hurt again."

Tears started to form in the corners of my eyes, but I didn't bother to reach up and wipe them, nor did I take my eyes off him.

"Last night was the first time in forever that you finally let the drawbridge down for visitors," he said with no humor in his voice.

I coughed. "If that's a euphemism—" I started to say, but he cut me off by rolling his eyes.

"It wasn't," he quickly said, "and yeah, maybe I should've picked a better metaphor, but it's still true." He sat back. "I give you a lot of credit for not going postal and mowing down half the town. I don't think I would've survived." He looked up at the ceiling. "If my boyfriend got killed in front of me and my best friend betrayed me, I would've been on the next bus to Arkham Asylum."

I sat there and stared at him. "Fuck. And I thought I was blunt."

He looked back at me, and I could tell he immediately regretted what he'd said. "Shit, I didn't mean for that to come off so dicky." He scratched his head with both hands rapidly, like it was going to help him turn back time and not say what he'd just said.

"No," I said. "Don't apologize for speaking the truth."

"Huh?" He stopped messing his already messy hair.

"You're right," I said, finally wiping my eyes with the sleeve of my shirt. "Everything has been built up so much that the floodgates finally broke open last night." He raised an eyebrow, and I sighed. "Yes, in more ways than one."

Sebastian laughed once, and I smiled at him.

"You know, aside from my lunatic family, there's only been one other person who's been able to crack this heart of ice." I tapped the middle of my chest.

"Oh?" he said, intrigued.

"Yeah, his name is Kyle," I said.

Sebastian looked like I'd punched him in the gut with a two-by-four.

"No, no, no!" I said quickly, "It's not like that. He's just a teenager."

Now Sebastian looked like I'd just started coughing up earthworms.

"*No!* It's not like that either!" I waved my hands in front of my disgusted face. "Ew! Really? You think I'm a pedophile? Gross."

"Well, how the hell do you expect me to react?" He threw his hands up in the air. "You just said that I reminded you of a teenager! That's all sorts of fucked-up."

I couldn't help but laugh; if Kyle were there at the moment, he would be acting the same way as Sebastian. "I'm just saying that he is too damn intuitive for his own good, and something tells me you got a fully functional brain behind that pretty face."

He raised an eyebrow at me. "Keep digging yourself deeper, Rob," he said, crossing his arms.

"You keep calling me that," I said.

"Keep calling you what?" he asked.

"Rob. No one's called me that in years."

"It's your name, isn't it?"

"Yeah, I guess," I said. "Or at least a form of it."

"Well, I like it better. It separates me from the rest of the pack," he said proudly. "Robbie is too cutesy for you." I shot him a look. "I'm not saying you're not cute!" he recovered. "Because you are." He moved his eyebrows up and down and wagged his tongue at me.

"You pig," I said with a touch of anger, even though I secretly loved it.

He laughed. "So tell me about this Kyle kid. What's his deal?"

"Hmm…. Kyle is a good egg," I said. "The short version of his tale is that he and his moose of a boyfriend, Brad, both came out of the closet in high school, had to deal with the suicide of their friend, survived an almost school shooting, the prom, and graduation."

Sebastian just stared at me. "What the fuck kind of a place did you live in?"

"I know," I sighed. "The 'almost' school shooting was what really brought Tyler and me back to speaking terms. In some sort of bizarre and twisted way, Kyle and Brad were the Mini-Me versions of the two of us, and we were very protective of them. We did everything in our power not to let another tragedy happen."

Sebastian sat there and said nothing.

I took a breath. "Now the boys are in California and dealing with life outside of Foster. I can only hope they don't get chewed up and spit out." I looked over at my phone on the nightstand, even though it didn't ring.

"So that's who you were on the phone with last night," Sebastian said, breaking me out of my trance.

"How did you know?" I looked at him curiously.

"I'm a light sleeper, and you're not exactly the quietest person I've ever met." He laughed when I turned red. "I figured out it was him from what you were saying."

"An eavesdropper?" I shook my finger at him. "Naughty, naughty."

"A big mouth?" He shook his finger right back at me and winked. "What happened to Tyler?"

"Oh, he has a moose of his own now." I thought about Matt.

"Wow. I didn't realize they had so many moose down in Texas," Sebastian said. "What kind of animal does that make me?"

"Umm… I'm thinking a reindeer, because even though you're big and dopey-looking, you're still kinda smart." I smiled a toothy grin.

"Thanks," he grumbled. "You know reindeer are better than people." He looked over at me as if I was going to give him a carrot.

I laughed and knew I could forgive him for missing every other reference I had made so far.

"What time is it?" He looked over at the clock on the microwave. "Shit, it's eleven already?"

I looked at the clock and then back at him. "Yeah, it is."

I knew what was coming next. He was going to leave after I'd just poured my guts out and never speak to me again.

"If you have to go…," I started.

"I'm starving," he continued, drowning out my words. "Let's go get some grub."

He took half a step toward me, put out his hands, palms up, and motioned with his fingers for me to put my hands in his.

"What am I? Eighty?" I groaned.

He pulled me out of the chair so fast that I lurched forward, almost hitting him in the chest.

"I certainly hope not," he said as he bent down until his face was two inches from mine. "I've heard of robbing the cradle, but robbing the walker is totally not my thing, because last night I may have broken your hip. Twice."

He smiled and kissed me softly as he grabbed my hips and I wrapped my arms around his neck.

He pulled away suddenly. "Oh, and you better stop smoking, because I'm not dating anyone who smells like an ashtray."

I rolled my eyes. "Really? Right now? Can we have breakfast before you start in on my bad habits, Mr. Cockatoo Hair?"

"Oh, are you jealous, baldy?" he asked and proceeded to smack my ass.

I gasped, "Fuck you very much!" and tugged at his golden-brown mop.

"What was that?" He turned his right ear toward me. "You want me to fuck you in the shower before we eat?"

I opened my mouth to argue, but he picked me up and started walking toward the bathroom before I could get a word out.

I supposed french toast could wait.

"YOU GONNA eat that?" Sebastian asked, mouth full as he reached stealthily toward me, his fork aimed at my plate.

Like a ninja, I grabbed his wrist with one hand and pulled the plate away from him with the other. "Don't. Touch. My. Bacon," I threatened, every word clear and spoken slowly. My warning was more of a death threat. Many have tried and failed to eat the one food I can't live without.

He slowly swallowed his third helping of raspberry-stuffed french toast. "Yes, sir," he said. "Can I have my eatin' hand back now?"

I let go of his wrist, and he pulled it to safety. "Sorry," I said, "but bacon's the gift from the gods I never share."

"I see," Sebastian said as he rubbed his arm. "I'll make sure to make a note of that for any future breakfasts together." He winked and scooped another bite of french toast into his mouth.

I shook my head and bit off a piece of my precious bacon.

"What?" he mumbled with food in his mouth again.

I sighed. "First of all, you eat like you just got out of prison, with the table manners to match. Secondly, what makes you so sure I want to have another breakfast with you?"

I mean, I totally did want to. And I totally wanted to have the prebreakfast adventures many times too.

Without missing a beat he said, "Because I like you."

I blushed a little and took a sip of my tomato juice to prevent myself from giggling.

"And by the color of your cheeks, I can tell you like me too," he added with a syrupy grin.

I put my glass down and stared at him for a second. "I do like you. A lot, actually, but we've known each other for—" I looked at the big clock behind the counter. "—not even twenty-four hours."

"So?" he said, taking another bite of food, this time a little more cautiously. "I'm not asking you to marry me or anything."

"I know, but—"

"You know, but what?" He set down his fork and wiped his mouth. "Rob, you're awesome and I like being around you. I don't need to go on twenty more dates to realize that."

I let a small smile appear on my face.

"I'm too old to play chicken with someone I like anymore. I'm tired of those kind of games. I like you, I want you to know it, so fuck it. And how many other times will I be able to tell people a first date began with dinner and someone punching me in the 'nads?" he added.

I started to laugh, and he chuckled just the least bit. "Not many, I would hope," I said.

"Exactly," he agreed and squeezed my hand.

I looked at his hand on top of mine and was about to check around to see if anyone was watching, but remembered we were far from any other customers.

"Besides," he said, "between your sister constantly raving about her sexy older brother at work and the past 'less than twenty-four hours,' I don't think there's much more I need to know about you."

I cringed at the thought of my sister talking about me. "I don't think Nicole would ever refer to me as 'sexy.'"

"All right, I put that part in there, but everything else she said about you is true." He gave my hand another squeeze before diving back into his almost demolished breakfast.

"Jesus Christ," I said, "do you live at the gym or do you take the bulimia express everywhere you go?"

"Very funny," he said. "I take care of myself enough so I can eat what I want. That's pretty much it."

"Interesting." I took another bite of bacon but put the rest down because I didn't exercise and I did eat like shit any chance I get. I pushed the plate away, suddenly losing my appetite.

"Why'd you stop eating?" he asked.

"Because I don't want you to think that I'm a fat bitch who sits at home and eats bacon-flavored everything all the time," I confessed.

"I didn't think that at all," he said as he stopped eating. "But I think that you think that I think it's going to turn me off if you did."

"I guess?" I said, now totally confused.

He paused and looked up as he reviewed his own sentence. "Okay, let me try again. Your first impression of me when I came to your door—not when I threw up on you at the bar, which doesn't count, by the way—was that I was some pretty-boy asshole who only liked guys who looked like me." He stared deep into my eyes. "Right?"

I stared back and wanted to lie, but what was the use?

"Right," I answered. "But you can't blame me, can you?"

"Why would you say that?" He leaned in to stare at me more, making me half embarrassed and half self-conscious and completely horny.

I sighed. "Because I've dealt with your kind before and it never ended well."

"I see," he said and took a sip of water. "Allow me to tell you a little story, then."

"Please do," I said with a wave of my hand. "I think it's time for me to learn a little more about the all-powerful Sebastian... wait. I don't even know your last name, yet you know my whole backstory, address, and six out of ten of my favorite sex positions."

What the fuck had just come out of my mouth?

His eyes got wider at that last part. "Hmm...." he muttered. "Only six, huh? I counted eight, but I suppose that one was just a variation of... yeah, okay, we'll have to rectify that. Soon."

He laughed while my face matched the tomato juice in my glass.

"Wyatt is my last name, but don't ask what I am," he said. "I'm a mutt according to my parents, and my family tree has so many branches that it should be a redwood." He took a big gulp of water. "I left home after I went to community college for one semester. I had some old football friends who got into UCLA, and they kept telling me I should come out there to visit."

"You played football in high school?" I asked.

"Yeah," he said.

"Of course you did," I said quietly. "Please continue."

He gave me a weird look but carried on. "Anyway, since I had some money left over from graduation, I decided to pack my bags and fly out to Cali. My buddies had an extra bed in the house they were staying at and said I could stay there for cheap. I was going nowhere fast here, so it didn't take much more than that to convince me."

"Been there," I said.

"At that point I was young and stupid and couldn't sit down for more than five minutes without wondering what else was going on in the world." He looked out the window. "Little did I know." He turned back to me. "Anyway, so I get out there and it's fun and keggers for the first month or so. Of course my ADD kicked in and I got bored with that. I needed a job, but I barely had any skills. So what does a barely out of the closet gay boy do? Yup. You guessed it. I waited tables.

"It was truly the glamorous life, let me tell you. I would work all day, then party all night. And sometimes I would squeeze an audition or two in there, because that's what you did if you were young, somewhat good-looking, and wanted quick money in LA.

"Half the time I would get so bombed the night before that if my manager hadn't had a crush on me, he would've fired me for coming in hungover every other day. I was a mess, but again I was young and stupid and didn't give two shits. It was drink or smoke, fuck, pass out, repeat.

"It went on for years like that. My parents kinda knew I was gay, but I never told them anything whenever I would come home for holidays. They thought I worked at an insurance company and lived with other young professionals and not a bunch of former jocks.

"One day this guy came into the restaurant I was working in West Hollywood and sat in my section. He was a good-looking guy and was only a couple of years older than me. My gaydar was fully developed by then, and I knew how to turn up the charm if I wanted to get a nice tip. I walked over to him and introduced myself, and he looked up from his menu and smiled at me with his shiny white veneers. He told me his name was Bryan Dupree and before I could ask what wine he wanted to go with his meal, he offered me a modeling job."

I rolled my eyes. "Of course he did," I said out of the corner of my mouth.

"Hey, I'm no Tyra Banks, but I do okay." I rolled my eyes and he asked, "May I continue, you sarcastic bitch?"

I glared at him. "Proceed."

"Thank you," he said, scratching the side of his nose with his middle finger. "So there began my short career in modeling and the beginning of my longest relationship."

"Wait, what?" I stopped him.

"Yeah, we ended up not only working together, but sleeping together," Sebastian admitted. "You see, Bryan was this big-shot up-and-coming designer, and his career was really starting to take off when we first got together. He was different than anyone I ever was with. Hell, his whole life was different from anything I was used to. I started off on the runway and ended up in the bedroom.

"Once we actually decided we were a couple, I stopped doing his fashion shows because models hate each other already with drag-queen-like levels, so I didn't want to give them a reason to look at me because I was sleeping with the boss.

"We kept our relationship somewhat quiet, with only a few friends knowing the whole story. I was pretty happy, and we traveled all over meeting celebrities and partying with them until dawn."

"What the hell made you come back here?" I asked as he took another sip of water.

"I didn't get there yet." He held up his hand.

"Sorry," I said. "Your drama sounds so much better than mine."

"Everyone's drama sounds better than your own. That is why reality TV is the 900-pound gorilla in the world right now."

I gave him a confused look. "There's a reality show about gorillas?"

"Ha. Ha," he said in a monotone.

"Fine, see if I'm nice to you next time you try your stand-up act. So you were dating the boss...," I said.

"Shit, where was I?" he scratched his head. "Did I get to the part where I came home one night and Bryan had not one, but two guys in our bedroom, apparently modeling his new invisible clothing line?"

"Oh fuck," I said.

"Yeah, that happened." Sebastian sighed. "And that wasn't even the worst part, though." He leaned back in the booth. "After I told him I was leaving, he went around and told people that I was only in it for the money. Which, believe me, was fucking bullshit, because any money he got went right down his throat or up his fucking nose. But since he was somewhat 'famous,' I got the short end of the stick and was shunned by any friends I'd made while we were together, because it's much easier to think the young guy is money-hungry rather than the older guy might be trading up to this year's model."

"Well, that certainly does suck," I said.

"You're telling me," he said. "I think I really did love him. I mean, did I like being pampered? Of course! Who wouldn't? I took whatever shit I cared about out of the house and moved into a motel for a week until I finally called up my mom and drove back out here. Cut to me working in a mailroom and living in my parents' basement, trying to figure out how to catch up with the life I was supposed to have already. If you asked me out of high school if ten years later I'd be living in the same room with my parents, making minimum wage, I would have told you to go fuck yourself. Yet here I am."

I sat there for a moment while Sebastian looked down at his empty plate.

"So, you see, I don't have the time to deal with bullshit anymore," he said as the waitress came by and took our dishes. "I know what I had, but I didn't sign up for that shit."

"I gotcha," I said.

"Yup," he responded.

"So how in the fuck did you get involved with Sean?" I had to ask because it had been bugging me ever since the disastrous dinner the night before.

"Ugh... him," he sighed. "After being back for a while, I decided that it was time to start meeting new people. I signed up for one of those retarded gay app things, and he contacted me within the first five minutes I was on."

"Ew, please don't tell me it was Grindr." I made a disgusted face.

He gasped and clutched his pretend pearls. "What kind of a slut do you think I am?"

"Umm... you kinda did have sex with someone you just met, like, ten hours ago, so...."

"Technically, it was the second time we met, and since I barfed all over you the first time, I figured I owed ya." He smiled like a jackass.

"Schmuck." I laughed.

"Anyway, he sent me this picture that obviously was twelve years and fifty pounds out of date," he explained. "I thought he was cute, so we decided to meet. All was cool until he said that he wanted to meet at Thunders. I should've said no right then and there, but I needed to get out more than just going to the gym."

"Yeah, you should really go more," I said and rolled my eyes.

"You think so?" He stretched his arms above his head. Every muscle popped out. "I think I let myself go."

A warm sensation erupted in the lower half of my body. "I hate you."

He lowered his arms and winked. "So I got to the bar at nine thirty and that fuck wasn't even there yet. There was a gaggle of good-looking guys staring at me while I ordered a beer from the bartender. I sat there and didn't pay them any mind, because just by their looks I could tell they were a bunch of assholes. Gay, stuck-up sharks circling the same water looking for chum to fuck. No matter what coast I'm on, I can tell a shit when I see one."

I laughed quietly because I shared a similar ability.

"As I milked my one beer quietly, I checked my phone and it was ten o'clock. I got up to leave when in marched the one-man pride parade," he said.

"Yup, that'd be Sean," I said.

"He walks right over to the group I was trying to avoid and screams, 'HEEEYYY GUUUURLS!!!'" Sebastian did a pretty spot impression and I almost fell out of the booth because I was laughing so hard.

"He went and gave everyone a stupid air kiss and told them he's meeting some guy named Sebastian. I wanted to crawl into a fucking hole and die when I heard my name." He grabbed his head with both hands and tried to scratch the memory out. "I swear I was going to ditch him because, number one, he was acting like a complete idiot, and number two, well, you've seen him."

I nodded my head.

"I'm not a shallow prick, but, dude, why send a pic of yourself if you look nothing like that?" He shook his head. "He didn't even sound like that when we talked on the phone! I hate fake people and I hate liars. I was used to it in LA—I mean, half the people there were either actors or wanted to be actors. Lying was, like, their life. But there was no way in gay hell I was going to deal with that here."

"Understandable," I said quietly.

"I was about to jet. Unfortunately he saw me react to my name and pranced right over to me since I looked like my damn picture." He made a *duh* face. "I tried my best to keep a smile on my mug when he dragged me over to meet his entourage of fags, which of course were the gay sharks I had been avoiding all night. I still have no idea what their names were, but after I met each one, he would turn to the others and say something under his breath." Sebastian made a fist with each hand. "I fucking hate that shit."

I put my hand on top of one of his and squeezed.

He looked up at me. "It was like everything I'd left in LA was starting over again. I was about to make the excuse that my cat died or something in order to leave when Sean came over with a drink in his hand." He shrugged. "A free drink was the least I deserved, so I downed it in one gulp. Sean looked somewhat horrified when I did it—and now I know why. It didn't take long for whatever was in there to kick in."

"Which is when I had the delight of meeting you," I said.

He laughed. "Yeah, you did. Sorry, in case I haven't already said I was. Though honestly, who shows up to a bar in a *Star Trek* shirt?"

I corrected him immediately. "It's *Doctor Who*, thank you."

I saw the smile spread across his face, and I knew I had been had. "Nerd" was all he said.

Ignoring that, I added, "The ride home in my underwear was kinda liberating, looking back on it now."

"Oh yeah?" He grabbed my hand and ran his fingers up my arms. "Wanna do it again?" He gave me a smoldering look.

"Check, please!" I yelled to our waitress.

Okay, so we didn't drive back to my place pantless.

We kept them on until we got back to my house, where all bets were off.

After another roll in the hay, Sebastian and I took another shower, which led to a swim in the hay, for lack of a better term.

If I were a rabbit, I would've mothered about 10,000 bunnies and had a bad limp by the end of the day.

Sebastian's clothes were a mess from being thrown around all over the house. I told him I would do a quick load of laundry.

"You want me to just sit around buck nekkid until they're done?" he asked, standing there completely nude. "I don't mind, and by the look of your pants, it doesn't seem you mind either." He smiled devilishly.

"No," I said, holding up my hand. "I'm good for the rest of the day—the rest of the week, actually. I'll get you something. Just go over there so I don't get tempted." I averted my eyes and pointed to somewhere on the other side of the house.

I went into my bedroom and dug through my closet and dresser for something that would fit Sebastian's larger frame. I quickly remembered I had something that might work and giggled evilly when I found the items.

I walked out of the bedroom and into the bathroom, doing the best I could not to look out of the corner of my eye at the figure dancing naked to my iPod in the middle of my living room.

I put the clothes on the counter and backed out the door. I turned around and closed my eyes. "Go put those on." I pointed—I think—to the bathroom.

"Yes, sirree, sir!" I heard Sebastian say. He rubbed his chest on mine and grabbed my ass on his way to get changed.

I reached out to smack him, but he closed the door before I could, making me hit my hand on the knob.

"That hurt, you dick!" I yelled, and I heard his deep laugh from the other side of the door.

You'll pay for that, I thought to myself.

I sat down on a chair and, as I waited for him to get dressed, I checked my phone to see that my sister had texted me three times in the past five minutes.

WHERE THE HELL ARE YOU?!

IS EVERYTHING OK?!

I'M AT MOM'S. I'M COMING OVER THERE IF I DON'T HEAR FROM YOU IN THE NEXT 10 MINUTES!

I was going to text her back when I heard Sebastian yell, "*What the fuck?*" and slam the bathroom door open.

Tears dripped from my eyes as I sat there laughing at the sight of him.

He stood like some sort of caveman, breathing heavily in an old pair of yoga pants that fit me fine but struggled to reach the floor on him. The oversized canary-yellow nightshirt with Belle and the words "Mornings Can Be Such a *Beast*!" on its front barely contained his wide chest.

"Are you fucking kidding me right now?" he hollered.

"Nope!" I said and raised my phone to take a quick picture. I looked at the image and almost started crying, I was laughing so hard.

"Delete that *now*," he ordered.

I pushed a few buttons on my phone. "What? I'm sorry, I was making that my profile pic."

His eyes flashed red like a matador's cape was being waved in front of him. "You're fucking dead!" He ran over and tackled me to the floor.

I would've struggled to get free, but I was laughing so much that it wouldn't have made a difference.

"Oh, so you think this is funny, do ya?" he said, and I could see he was about to crack at any second. He held my hands down with one of his. "I'll give you something to laugh about!"

I tried to stop laughing, but it was no use since he was tickling me with his free hand.

At that moment my sister Nicole burst through my front door.

"Robbie!" she screamed and proceeded to jump on Sebastian's back. "You get off my brother, you fucknut!"

"Nicole!" I yelled from under Sebastian, who barely registered my sister's weight. "I'm fine!"

"No you're not!" she screamed back as she wrapped her legs around Sebastian and accidentally—or on purpose—kicked him right in the balls.

He fell right on top of me like a bag of rocks with an extra bag on top of him.

"Get. Off," I struggled to yell at the both of them.

"Oh shit!" Nicole said and she stood up quickly. "Robbie, are you okay?"

"Noooo...." I gasped as I rolled the now moaning Sebastian off me.

"Shit," Nicole said and helped me up.

"Really?" I pointed to Sebastian, who was rocking back and forth holding on to his crotch.

"You didn't answer my text!" she shouted, as if that was enough validation for her. "And then I came in here and he's on top of you and... wait a sec. Is that my nightshirt?" She crouched down to look closer. "I knew you took it!" She glared menacingly back at me. "You told me you hadn't seen it!"

"Oh, shut up, Nicole. You left it at my house the last time you came down to visit me, and possession is nine-tenths of the law," I retorted. "Besides, whatever happened to my leather jacket in high school? The one that looked like George Michael's from 'Faith'? Where could that have gone?"

We argued back and forth until a voice below us said, "No… really. I'm fine. Uuuughhh…."

Nicole and I stopped fighting and leaned down to lift him onto the couch. Of course he weighed like he was secretly a robot in disguise, so we got him halfway onto it and he heaved himself up the rest of the way.

"Thanks," he said to both of us as he tried to swallow his testicles back down for the second time in two days.

"Sorry about your nuts, Sebastian," Nicole said, embarrassed.

He took a deep breath. "It's fine, Nic. Just please don't tell me you have any other family members who want to play kick the can with my balls."

Of course that's when my mother, wearing a bright pink caftan, dashed through the door.

"What the hell is going on here?" she asked. "I heard Nicole scream." Her eyes fell on Sebastian, and I could swear I saw his hands cover his crotch.

"Just a misunderstanding, Ma," I said as I sat down next to Sebastian on the couch.

"Yes, Mother," Nicole said. "I'm glad you came running so quickly." She rolled her eyes and plopped down on the love seat.

My mother folded her arms. "I am in the middle of making dinner, Nicole, or did you forget that you invited yourself over tonight?" She arched an eyebrow.

"No." Nicole shrank back farther into the couch.

My mother gave her a quick nod, then looked over at Sebastian and me. She unfolded her arms and walked over to us with a big smile.

"You must be Sebastian," she said as she stuck out her hand palm side down in front of him.

I closed my eyes and counted to three.

Nope, they were all still there.

"Nice to meet you, Mrs. DeCaro." Sebastian shook her hand. "I would get up to greet you properly, but I'm having a little trouble standing right now."

"Oh?" she said. "Ohhhhh…." She looked at me and winked.

"Mother!" I yelled. "Not that! Nicole kicked him in the balls!"

"Nicole Marie! Why would you do that?" she scolded her.

"I thought…. Ooh, never mind!" She got up off the couch and headed toward the door. "Ma, let's go. I think your sauce is boiling over."

"Oh shit," my mother said and followed my sister to the door. She turned back to us and said, "Sebastian, honey?"

"Yes, Mrs. DeCaro?" he replied politely.

"Rose, please," she said, and he nodded. "You are more than welcome to stay for dinner. My brother, James, will also be joining us."

He perked up at mention of food as if all the pain had evaporated from his body. I was about to protest when Sebastian said, "That would be lovely, Miss… I mean, Rose. Thank you."

She smiled and pinched Nicole on her arm to move. "Isn't that your shirt?" she said to Nicole as she slowly closed the door behind them.

I watched them leave and turned back to look at Sebastian, who had a shit-eating grin on his face.

"You better leave while you still can," I pleaded with him. "I'll FedEx your clothes."

"I think she likes me," he said and batted his eyes.

I rolled mine. "We'll see," I said and got up off the couch. "Just pretend to like her sauce even if you don't. Otherwise you'll be leaving here tonight in a body bag."

Chapter Six
No Escape from the Storm Inside of Me

AS MUCH as I wanted my uncle to see him dressed like he should be riding the short bus, Sebastian insisted on wearing his own clothes to dinner.

"But they're still damp!" I protested when he reached into the dryer.

He shook out any wrinkles from his shirt. "You've had enough laughter at my expense tonight, Rob."

I waved him off. "Whatever you say," I lowered my voice, "Seb." I didn't think "Sebby" would've gone over too well since that asshole Sean had called him that.

"Seb?" He paused before putting on his shirt. "That's a new one." He smiled. "I like it!"

I laughed. "Bastian would've just sounded weird coming out of my mouth."

"And it would constantly remind me of that scary movie," he said as he put his pants and socks on.

"What scary movie?" I asked.

"You know, the one from the eighties about the kid and the book and the scary dog-dragon thing." His body shook like he'd gotten a chill.

"*The NeverEnding Story?*"

"That's it!" He pointed at me. "That's some scary shit right there."

"You're scared of *The NeverEnding Story*?" I laughed. "You can't be serious. Next thing you'll tell me is that you're scared of *The Goonies* too." I giggled some more.

Seb's face turned bright red.

I stopped laughing. "Holy shit, you're scared of that too?" The laughing started again.

"Shut up!" he yelled. "That pointed-headed guy freaks me out!"

I was practically on the floor, rolling around in a hysterical fit, and he just stood there like a kid whose ice-cream cone had fallen to the sidewalk.

My text message alert went off and I got up, trying to control my laughter. "Okay, okay," I said to him. I picked up the phone and read the message from my mother.

DINNER! DON'T FORGET TO WASH YOUR HANDS!

"We have to go anyway." I smiled up at him even though he still pouted. "Let's go eat. That'll make you feel better." I stood on my tiptoes and gave his cheek a kiss.

He tried to stay mad, but I was pretty sure the mention of food would magically change his entire disposition. "Fine," he sighed. "If we have to."

He looked down at me with a furrowed brow, and I gave him a pearly smile. He squinted, and I knew it had worked.

"Bitch," he quietly muttered.

"Asshole," I responded. "Okay, let's go. Let me just make sure everything is turned off and locked up."

He tilted his head. "We're going to be twenty feet away. Why are you worried about locking the door?"

"Because" was all I said.

He waited there for a minute for an answer, I assumed, but I was too busy checking everything was safe and tight before I said, "Okay," and headed for the door.

"After you," I announced gallantly. As he passed I may have pinched him on his left butt cheek, but I assure you it was an accident.

I locked the door behind me and grabbed Sebastian's hand for the less-than-thirty-second walk to my mother's back door.

"You ready?" I asked him.

"Definitely," he said. "My stomach is open for business."

He stopped after realizing I wasn't moving.

"What's wrong?" he asked.

"I meant are you ready to have dinner with my family?" I said.

"Yeah, why?" he said, completely unfazed. "Why wouldn't I be? I already know Nicole, and your mom seemed to like me. Plus didn't you say that your big gay uncle is a pisser?"

I had said that. Uncle James could make a dirty joke at a morgue and people would laugh.

"All right," I said, still a little unconvinced.

Seb saw the hesitation in my eyes and pulled me close. "Hey," he whispered, "it's cool. You know how many dinners like this I got dragged to in high school? Trust me, parents love me."

He lowered his head and gave me a gentle kiss.

I closed my eyes and enjoyed it until I saw the patio lights being turned on and off over and over. I broke away from Seb's mouth to peer in the window. Nicole stood there, waving her hands like a moronic little sister and mouthing the words "I'm hungry."

"Remind me to beat her later," I said, and Sebastian laughed.

"I am not getting involved in violent situations with any member of your family again without a cup. Thank you very much," he said.

"Fine," I sighed.

We walked up the deck stairs, and I opened the sliding glass door that led right into my mother's kitchen.

She was busy stirring a pot of pasta while simultaneously adding spices to another pot that contained her tomato sauce. To this day I still have no idea how she made everything taste perfect.

The sound of someone's stomach grumbling next to me broke my mother's concentration, and she turned to look at us with a wooden spoon in her hand.

Like many products of Italian households, I had a quick flashback to my childhood and my mother scolding me with a wooden spoon in hand for backup if her words didn't get the point across. She only had to put her hand on the drawer where it was stored away and my attitude would change immediately.

However, at that moment my mother couldn't look less threatening.

She smiled at Nicole and me. "Good, you're here. Robert, help your sister finish setting the table."

"Sure, Ma," I replied and walked over to the cabinet where Nicole was taking out plates and utensils like it was killing her.

"Thank you," my mother said. She looked at Sebastian, who was standing there probably feeling completely out of place. "And Sebastian? Could you be a dear and please help me with draining this pasta? My carpal tunnel is acting up and I can't lift the heavy pot."

"No problem," he replied, smiling politely.

Nicole and I looked at each other.

"Since when does Ma have problems with her wrists?" I whispered.

"Since never," Nicole responded. "You know this is what she does."

I grunted in response, thinking about the time I first brought Riley home to meet my mother. I think she made him take out the garbage within five minutes after we got there.

"Oh, excellent," my mother praised as Sebastian drained the last of the pasta in the sink. "Now if you wouldn't mind, could you grab me that bowl over on the counter?" She pointed to the large glass container across the room.

"I'll get it," I said and mouthed the word "Stop" to her while Sebastian's back was turned.

Naturally she flipped me off.

As I brought her the bowl, I heard the front door open and close followed by the pitter-patter of a middle-aged gay man's feet.

"Hello, hello, hello!" James called as he walked into the kitchen. "The party has arrived!" He held up a bottle of white wine. "Sorry I'm running a little late, Rose, but the traffic was horrendous!"

"You live down the road, you twit," she said as she gave him a kiss on the cheek and took the bottle of wine. "Go sit."

"Yes, ma'am," he said with a salute, and she playfully hit him on his shoulder. "Hello, children." He blew a kiss to Nicole and me as we finished setting the table. "Ooh, Robbie! How did your date go last night? Did ya get some?"

My face turned pale and my mouth dropped open.

Sebastian stopped washing his hands in the sink and turned off the water. James couldn't see him until he walked over where I was standing. "What's wrong?" my uncle asked and then saw Sebastian standing there grinning awkwardly.

"Hi there," he said to my uncle and stuck out his hand. "I'm Sebastian."

James laughed quietly and walked over to place his hand into Sebastian's.

I inched closer to both of them as a precaution.

"*Enchanté*," my uncle said like he worked in the Moulin Rouge.

Sebastian look confused but smiled anyway.

James looked at me. "Big boy, isn't he?" he asked while still shaking Sebastian's hand.

My eyes opened wide, but before I could fry my uncle's head with lasers, my mother called out, "Dinner's ready!"

James let go of Sebastian's hand. "I'll be right there, Rose," he said and turned back to Sebastian. "Would you excuse my nephew and me for a moment? He needs to look at something I found on my back, and I wouldn't want to scare you."

Sebastian looked even more confused and nodded before going to the table, while I stood there turning red.

"Thank you, Sebastian," James said with a strange smile. He grabbed me by my elbow and dragged me into the living room. "What the hell do you think you're doing?" he said, finally letting go when we were out of sight.

"First of all, ow." I rubbed my throbbing forearm. "Secondly, what are you talking about?"

"Why is he still here?" he whispered. "Wasn't your date last night?"

"Ma invited him this morning!" I said. "You know her and her need to feed everyone."

"This morning?" He looked like he was going to blow. "You mean he hasn't left yet?"

"Yeah. So?" I shrugged.

"So again I ask," he said, "why is he still here?"

I crossed my arms, getting pissed. "Weren't you the one who told me I needed to get out and get my legs back up in the air?"

"Yes," he snapped, "but I wanted you to dip your toe in the pool, not dive headfirst into the ocean!"

I shook my head at him. "Can we talk about this later? I'm starving, and I don't need a lecture about the etiquette of one-night stands from you right now."

He sighed and dropped his shoulders. "Fine, I'm just making sure you don't put all your horny eggs in one basket on the first guy you go on a date with in five years." He waved his hands like a fashion magazine editor. "To be continued," he crooned before walking back into the kitchen.

He left me there speechless.

I shook it off, walked to the counter, grabbed the bottle of wine my uncle had brought, and opened it in record time. I filled the nearest glass and took a drink, not bothering to ask anyone else if they wanted some.

My mother dropped a pound of pasta on Sebastian's plate, exclaiming "You're too thin!" and squeezed his cheek. She looked at me and winked.

I smiled, knowing she only wanted to see me happy and would do anything in her power not to fuck that up. Even if it meant inviting a guy to dinner after we'd been on one date.

My Uncle James was a different story. The usually crass and hilarious man was replaced by someone I didn't recognize. His posture seemed too stiff and the expression on his face was a mix of annoyance and disgust. On anyone else I would have called it jealousy, but I knew James better than that. He was mentally circling the wagons, which meant he was about to go on the attack.

I placed the wine bottle on the table and sat next to Sebastian, who was already halfway through his rigatoni. My mother sat at the head of the table to the left of me, which was rare because she barely stayed in one spot for more than two minutes during dinnertime just in case someone needed another helping of food. She constantly worried that there wasn't enough grated cheese or that someone needed something to drink. Tonight she stayed put to keep a careful eye on my uncle; she had seen the look too.

Nicole was across from me and next to Uncle James, who was curiously watching Sebastian shovel the food into his mouth.

Sebastian must've felt James staring, because he looked up and smiled. He wiped the sauce from the sides of his mouth and turned to my mother. "It's delicious, Rose," he said with a closed-mouth smile.

"Thank you," she said with a nod.

"Rose?" James repeated. "First-name basis already? That's new." He tilted his gaze toward his sister, who raised an eyebrow, but then continued to pick at his dinner.

I turned to Sebastian who sat there, quietly uncomfortable, then to an uncle I never had seen before. I gave him a look that said *What the fuck?* and he just smirked, daring me to say something in front of everyone.

"So, Sebastian—" My mother broke the gloomy silence. "—Nicole tells me that you work in the office with her. How is it there?"

"It's not bad," he said. "I like it, but I definitely don't want to be sorting mail for the rest of my life." He laughed.

My mother laughed with him. "No, I suppose that could get boring after a while."

Nicole and I glanced at each other and smiled. We mentally high-fived each other, knowing that Sebastian was winning her over.

I raised an eyebrow at James, who sat there blank-faced. "Such a shame that so much beauty is locked away all day instead of shining out in the sunlight," he said as he took a sip of wine.

Thinking James had made a lighthearted joke, Sebastian laughed politely and glanced at my mother, Nicole, and me to see if we were in on it. When he saw that we had all stopped laughing, he shut his mouth and went back to eating.

James grabbed the bottle of wine and poured some into the glass in front of him. He offered some to Sebastian.

"No, thank you." Sebastian waved his hand and shook his head. "I have to drive later."

"Oh," James said. "You weren't planning on staying another night at the fabulous Château de Robbie Bed & Breakfast?"

"James," my mother said, "why don't you shove some food in that big fat mouth of yours?" Her tone was more of a command than a request.

"Rose," he fired back at her, "our mother has been dead for ten years. Stop trying to be her."

The whole room got five degrees chillier.

"Now," he continued, "I want to hear more about our new friend, Sebastian, here."

Sebastian straightened his back and squared his shoulders. He wiped his mouth with his napkin and placed it on the table. He smiled broadly at James and asked, "What is it that you would like to know?"

If James was going to play ball, it seemed Sebastian had his bat ready.

Shit. Did I just use a baseball reference?

Fucking Tyler....

James smiled at him. "You came back from California, huh? Living there must've been like swimming in a pool of mirrors."

"Really, James?" I said and placed my fists on the table; I was about to get up in order to smack my uncle.

Sebastian placed his hand on top of mine.

Everyone's stares shot to the small public display of affection.

My uncle raised an eyebrow.

"I'm not sure what that means," Sebastian said, not taking his hand off mine, "but the reason I moved back here was because

I found a lot of people who liked judging other people on little to no information. At first I thought it was a West Coast thing, but now I'm thinking it might be a gay thing."

James leaned back with his wine glass in hand. "Huh. Interesting. Must get tiresome being surrounded by so many people who misunderstand you." He looked down at his plate and played with his food.

I practically growled, and Sebastian squeezed my hand tighter. I looked over at him and he gave me a nod that said *I got this*. Then he winked at me.

"Sebastian." My mother broke the silence and Sebastian's grasp. "Nicole tells me that you're living back with your parents in Amityville."

Thank you, Mother, for changing the subject.

"Yes," Sebastian answered with a bit of relief in his voice. "It's just temporary until I can figure out what I'm doing."

"Oh?" my uncle said. "I thought you've been back for over a year, from what Nicole has told me. How much longer do you need to figure it out?"

My sister's face went red. I was pissed that she'd told James a lot about Sebastian. Then I felt bad, because how could she have known he was going to be a bitch and bring it up in front of everyone?

Sebastian cleared his throat. "Yes, well, it's been difficult to find an apartment that I could afford, so I've been saving up to find a place that doesn't look like a serial killer stores the bodies in it."

We all giggled nervously at his joke except James, who never stopped smiling the same strange way.

"Well, at least you had someplace a little more... comfortable to sleep last night." He took one final gulp of wine.

I grabbed the bottle and emptied the contents into my own glass before he could have another drink. "Oops," I said, "All gone." I smiled innocently, which seemed like it pissed James off. He wasn't drunk, but I didn't want him to keep flapping his gums under the influence.

"You need it more than I do, I'm sure," he said to me. "Helps to calm those nerves of yours." James turned to Sebastian.

"This kid was always a nervous Nelly. And it's only become worse with age. Did he tell you about that during the five seconds you've known each other?"

Sebastian didn't respond. Instead he stared at me, his expression one of open and growing concern. I felt my heart beat faster. I took another gulp of alcohol and then a deep breath.

"No, we didn't discuss anything about that, and I really don't think this is an appropriate conversation to have right now." I almost growled. I felt my body temperature rise and knew it wasn't only due to the wine.

"I'm just saying." James waved me off. "It's not every day you get to have a free dinner with the family of a one-night stand."

If there were a record player spinning in the background, this is the part where the needle would scratch across the vinyl.

I heard the disgust in my mother's tone when she snapped my uncle's name. Nicole quietly mumbled, "Jesus Christ."

My mouth went numb since I was too shocked to say anything. Even James realized he had just fucked up royally, from the paleness of his face.

Sebastian let out a single laugh, wiped his mouth, and placed his napkin next to his dish. He turned to my mother and said, "Thank you so very much for dinner, but I'm afraid I must go." He smiled at my sister. "Nicole, I'll see you at work on Monday?" She nodded. He looked at James. "Thank you for a little slice of LA."

James seemed like he was going to say something, but Sebastian turned to me.

"Can you walk me out?" Sebastian asked me.

"Yeah," I said as I got up from the table.

When Sebastian was out of the room, I turned and glared at everyone but made sure I aimed a laser-sharp gaze at my uncle, letting him know full well this wasn't over. "To be continued," my ass.

Sebastian was standing by his car when I walked out of my mother's front door.

"I'm so sorry," I apologized. "I'm so, so sorry."

He shrugged. "It's not your fault. I just didn't want to stick around and be given the third degree anymore."

"I don't know what got into him. He's never like this," I tried to explain.

"He's protective of his nephew, that's all." He shrugged slightly, so innocently.

"Huh?" I said.

"Look at what happened tonight. Your uncle showed up thinking he was having dinner with his family, but then this stranger was sitting at the dinner table holding his nephew's hand." Sebastian grabbed my hand as reference. "Who, by the way, he only met the night before. It would weird me out too."

"So why did you leave?" I asked.

"Because I wasn't going to argue with someone who obviously loves you very much." He rested one hand on my shoulder. "If this," he pointed back and forth between me and him, "goes anywhere, I'm not going to start it all with me having a battle with your uncle."

I swallowed hard. I had no fucking idea what "this" was at that particular moment either, but after James's response, it was starting to worry me.

"Besides, I respect my elders." His serious tone faded and he smiled. "I don't think you should tell him I said that."

I laughed. "I won't. Don't worry."

"Please apologize to your mom and thank her again for dinner," he added.

"I will."

He smiled and pressed his hand to the side of my face. "You okay?" The same concern I'd seen in Sebastian's expression while I was talking about Riley had reappeared.

I didn't realize I had zoned out for a second, but Sebastian did.

"What?" I said. "Oh yeah. I'm fine."

He looked at me, unsure, but said, "Cool," with a smile.

"Sorry, my head is a little wonky," I said. "You should go. I mean, I should get back in there. I mean, you know what I mean?"

He looked like I'd punched him in the groin again. "Okay, then. Can I least get a kiss before I go?"

I smiled slightly. He pulled me close and leaned down to kiss me deeply.

While it was nice, I secretly hoped it wouldn't end.

He pulled away and grinned. "Until next time," he said with a hand squeeze and got into his car.

I watched him pull out of the driveway and stood there motionless when he honked the Jeep's horn and sped down the block.

The sounds of my mother, my uncle, and my sister screaming at each other brought me around and sent me running back to the house. I swung open the door just in time to hear James say, "Well, what the hell was I supposed to say?"

I slammed the door behind me and everyone shut up immediately.

"What were you supposed to say?" I snarled. "How about something that wasn't *rude*? What the fuck were you thinking?"

"Excuse me?" he said. "I was thinking that my nephew was acting like a complete schmuck bringing a trick to a family dinner. That's what!"

"James!" my mother yelled. "That was completely uncalled for! I invited Sebastian! Don't blame Robbie."

"Ma, don't get involved," Nicole said and pulled my mother into the kitchen.

"He didn't have to accept," he muttered. "Probably was waiting for a doggy bag too."

"What the hell is that supposed to mean?" I asked. My head was starting to spin because I was so angry.

"Oh, come on, Robbie. Do I have to spell it out for you?" he said. "He's charming, adorable, mooches off his parents, and now he's found someone whose family is financially comfortable. Give me a break!"

"So when Nicole set up a blind date with him, what do you think he did? Ask her for my W-2? He had no idea who I was before last night," I screamed. "Far be it from me to think that he actually liked me or something."

"You just said it, he had no idea last night and still doesn't. Nor do you know him, I might add," he spat back. "Just because you had a roll in the hay doesn't mean that you and this guy are going to fall in love. You just fucking met!"

"Really, Elsa? I'm not allowed to fall in love with a man I just met?" I asked, the sarcasm dripping off my words like venom. "Who's the Ice Queen now?" He squinted at me. "By the way, when did I ever say that I loved him or even that we were dating?"

"You didn't," he said, "but I know you. You have all that longing and loneliness inside of you that's been building up for years." He closed his eyes and shook his head. "And you. You just let it all out on the first guy you met? You should know better than that. This isn't some fairy tale." For a split second, his face looked like it aged twenty years.

"I never claimed it was," I said shakily as my body started to tighten. If I didn't calm down, I knew what was coming. I was riding the edge of a panic attack the same way a surfer tried desperately to stay ahead of a tidal wave.

"I have to say this because someone needs to," he said. "He isn't Riley."

I'm still not sure what came first, the spots in front of my eyes or the sound of the plate crashing in the kitchen. All I do know is that there were voices saying "How could you?" "He's going to lose it," and "I'm sorry. I didn't mean to say it!" I waved them out of the way, lurched forward, and ran out my mother's sliding glass door.

The roar of the crashing wave chased me all the way across the yard.

I jogged quickly around to my house and opened the door, closing it gently behind me. I locked it and turned off all the lights just so they'd know I didn't want to be bothered.

I looked at the clock on the cable box and started counting in my head as the time went by. I took two pills, quickly pulled my contacts out, put on my pajamas, and went straight to my bedroom. For all I knew, my mom and Nic were pounding on my door to open up; I couldn't hear anything over the roar of an angry ocean coming down on me. All the time I kept counting in my head.

I put my phone on mute, crawled under the covers that still had a Sebastian scent to them, and willed myself not to scream.

I closed my eyes and breathed deeply, trying desperately to fall asleep before the attack took over my body.

Chapter Seven
Conceal, Don't Feel, Defy Gravity

I WOKE up the next day around eleven to the sound of my phone vibrating on my nightstand. I picked it up before it shook itself to the floor. My eyes focused on the screen, and I saw it was a text from Sebastian.

Morning sunshine. Hope u had a good night. Sorry again 4 bailin'. TTYL ;)

I didn't reply, and my body ached when I stretched to drop the phone on my nightstand. My head felt like it was in a vise, and I desperately needed some water. I called it my "panic hangover." It would take me a bit to recover, especially since I'd slept after having the attack. My mind slowly readjusted itself after I got up and gulped another Xanax to ease the aftershocks.

I lay back down on my bed and picked up my phone.

Hey you. Totally understood why you left. Prolly should've gone with. Lol My stomach is not feeling well right now (too much pasta) so I'll talk to you soon ok? :)

Within seconds he wrote back *Kewl :) Peace out yo* and included a picture of him with his hand crooked into a gang sign.

I smiled slightly and dropped my phone on the bed.

I didn't have the stomach flu, and I had barely eaten anything last night. No, my sickness was something far worse, something I had thought I was finally getting over.

When my Uncle James had told Sebastian about my "nervous Nelly" condition at dinner, I knew having an attack was pretty inevitable. I was back in a situation I couldn't control and

I'd lost it. Sure, I could've told my uncle to shut the hell up or explained to Sebastian what he was talking about, but once I'd made a slight turn off the main highway and started driving down Panic Boulevard, my internal GPS shut down.

And James was right; things got worse with age.

I knew it was silly to be lying there feeling like shit for myself. I didn't want the cycle to start all over again. However, I knew it had. Those evil trolls living in the back of my brain were starting to get loud again after being silent for such a long time.

Were they trying to warn me about Sebastian? That maybe the attacks, both panic and from my uncle, were signs that he was bad news? Or that he'd just leave in some form like Riley had?

Overthinking every situation was too much to handle, so I pulled the covers over my head and went back to sleep.

I was a zombie the next few days. My sleeping pattern was completely off, and I barely ate. I smoked like a chimney and smelled like one too. I still hadn't spoken to Sebastian, and I was planning on keeping it that way. My sister texted me a couple of times to make sure I was okay and asked if she could stop by. I said I wasn't up for visitors.

I didn't want her to see me like this again.

She didn't press the issue and said to text her when I was feeling better. She wasn't dumb and probably knew what had happened to me after what Uncle James said.

I still hadn't heard from him either, and I had no plans to contact him ever again. When I would walk outside to smoke— and to let my mother see that I was still alive—I never saw his car in the driveway. What he'd said had hurt, and every time I thought about it, I would feel sick to my stomach.

The panic attack set me back on a downward spiral I thought I'd finally broken free of.

On Friday night, finally sick of being a stinky bitch, I dragged myself to the bathroom and took a long, hot shower. Half an hour later, as I was only partially covered in a towel, I headed back toward my bedroom at the same time my mother came through my front door, scaring the ever-loving shit out of me.

"Ma!" I screamed. "Naked!" I pulled my towel tighter around my body and ran for my bedroom.

"Oh, please," she yelled back. "I made you. I know what you look like naked."

"Gross!" I whined as I put on some random outfit and came out of the bedroom. She was going through my kitchen, checking the refrigerator and putting in food from the two bags I hadn't noticed since I was too busy running naked away from her. "What do you want, woman? And what is all this?"

She stopped long enough to look me up and down. "You're too thin." She went back to stockpiling my fridge.

"Of course I am," I muttered. "It's a new diet I'm doing. It's called the 'Robbie is starting to get panic attacks again and doesn't want to function' diet." There was no use giving her an excuse or lying to her. She was my mother, and mothers always knew when their kids were bullshitting them. "I think it's working quite nicely." I spun around as if I were on the runway.

She slammed the refrigerator door closed, and the glass jars inside all clanked together. "I don't think you're funny in the slightest." Her voice was level, but it still scared me, as if she were screaming at me. "You and Nicole make your smartass jokes thinking you're both the funniest thing on Long Island; well, you're not. It's an excuse to cover that you're falling apart inside and you know it." She took a deep breath and added, "You're doing it again."

I looked at her and said nothing.

"You're secluding yourself from everyone." She rubbed her forehead. "I can't let you get like this again."

I sat on a kitchen chair and looked at the floor. "I know."

She walked over, pulled out another chair, and sat in front of me. "When your father died, you were so young and so confused. You didn't understand death and how someone can be here one day, then gone the next."

I started to tear up as she continued.

"For so many years, you would worry every time I left the house or when James and Andy drove their car a hundred miles away for a vacation. You didn't want anything bad to happen to them like it had to your father. You never left the house because you were content with being alone. Do you remember that?"

I nodded, still not looking up at her.

"I thought it was because you were an independent kid, but in reality, you were scared of going out in the world and meeting new people," she said. "You didn't want to lose someone again."

That fear of loss was yet another reason why I didn't really have many friends growing up. I was shy to begin with—and then there was that whole playing with two Ken dolls that detracted from any sort of kinship.

"When did you get your doctorate, Dr. DeCaro?" I looked at her with tears in my eyes and a small smile.

"I am your mother," she said. "I know everything." She smiled back at me. "Of course, that all changed when you turned eighteen. All those fears melted away once you graduated high school and those hormones started to kick in." I made a disgusted face. "You were out at college and I was the one who had to worry all the time. Not you."

Scary, but true. I was a little twink having the time of my life. I hadn't bothered thinking consciously about negative things like death anymore. I learned to contain my anxieties beneath the business of college life, Broadway shows, and gallons of booze. I was out living the life I had thought I was going to live for years to come.

"I thought I was hot shit, didn't I?" I asked.

"You certainly did," she said with a laugh; then her face went still. "It all changed with Riley."

My eyes started to water again. "It certainly did."

She reached over and squeezed my hand.

"He never knew," I said to her.

She shot me a confused look.

"He never knew about my 'issues.' Or at least I don't think he knew."

When Riley and I had fallen in love and he'd become my world, you would've thought my negative thoughts or feelings would have finally dissipated.

Nope. His presence had just made the anxiety come galloping back into my life. I'd held it at bay as best as I could with medication and good friends.

"There was no reason for Riley to know about my darkened past since I was happy with him, and that was that," I said. "He didn't have to know about all those nights that I would lie awake because my brain just wouldn't shut off thinking about grocery lists, whether all the doors were locked, or all the times I'd look at him sleeping and think about when he was going to eventually leave me."

I'd thought he was going to leave me for Tyler, not get mowed down in front of me.

"You had attacks at least three times a day for two straight weeks after Riley died," my mother recalled. "I stayed with you until you were able to be part of society again. I knew you were feeling better because you practically kicked me out and threw the plane ticket at me."

"I did not," I said.

"Okay, maybe I exaggerated a bit."

"Ya think?" I asked.

She shrugged and I put my hand on top of hers. "You know how grateful I still am for that, right?"

She nodded. "Well, that makes sense. If you had told me then you were keeping it from him, we would have had this talk earlier. Anyway, I am your mother, so that means I can say things like this and it not be as horrible as it sounds."

My body tensed up. If up to this point she had been editing herself, I could not imagine what was coming next.

"You did Riley wrong," she said flatly.

And I'd thought what James said had hurt.

"You did him and yourself wrong by not telling him what you were going through, and I think I know why. You were scared of chasing him off or some garbage, which comes back to you being afraid of people leaving you, but in the end you, my dear boy, are an idiot."

Wow, she *had* been holding back all this time.

"Marriage." She paused. "No, not just marriage—love, period, is about sharing. You don't keep the bad things away from the one you love; you show it to them in all its terrible glory. Relationships, real ones, shouldn't be so fragile that the other one bolts at the first sign of trouble. Riley wouldn't have run away from you, and you know it."

Tears were falling down my face as I nodded.

"He could have helped you, and maybe he was hiding something too. God knows now. But being in love, real love, isn't a contest. It's not about who has the least amount of problems. There are no winners or losers. You both should get to the finish line at the same time. You should have told him."

I broke down and started to sob, and she moved over and hugged me as if I was nine years old and that horrible Max Phillips across the street had pulled the head off my Wonder Woman doll again. There were no words, no coherent thoughts. There was just pain that radiated from the center of me and just kept gushing out like....

Well I was going to say pus from a zit, but ewww.

"I don't know what is going on with this Sebastian boy," she said after a while. "But let me give you some free advice." I looked up at her. "Tell him. Tell him everything. If he runs away, then you know he wasn't the one."

"Then I'd be alone."

She gave me a small smile. "You'd be alone and free. You don't need anyone like that in your life."

I was ready for her to start editing herself again any moment.

"And I still am here for you," she said softly. "But this time I'm only fifty feet away and not 3,000 miles, so you're going to have to deal with it."

I got up and hugged her. "Thanks, Ma."

"That's what I'm here for," she said. "I love you."

"Love you too," I said back and let her go.

"Now," she said in a weird motherly tone, "speaking of this Sebastian...."

"Ma, don't," I protested. "I don't want to talk about it. It's done. You don't have to tell me things were going too fast and everything. I think Uncle James made that perfectly clear."

"I wasn't going to say any of that." She crossed her arms. "And what my brother says does not have any bearing on what I think or say. Screw him."

I looked at her and could tell she was very serious.

"I want nothing more in this world than to see my children happy," she said. "So what if you just met the kid? I knew that asshole I married after your father died for years, and look how well that turned out."

She was right.

"Your sister would not want you to meet someone who wasn't worthy of her brother. She loves you too much," she said. "Plus I raised you both well, so I'll take credit where credit is due."

I smiled and rolled my eyes.

"Does he make you laugh?" she asked.

I nodded.

"Does he make your stomach feel mushy?"

I laughed and nodded.

"And most importantly." She leaned in. "Does he like my cooking?"

I sighed. "Yes, Ma, he loved it."

"Then he's perfect!" she said, throwing her hands in the air.

I shook my head. "I don't know about that."

She stood up and walked over to me. "You're absolutely right. Neither do I. It could turn out like shit, but how are you going to know if you don't do anything about it?"

I looked at her and she waited for an answer. "I know, but…."

"No 'buts'!" She smacked me on the arm. "I'm not getting any younger and I want grandchildren, goddammit. Let's get a move on!"

I gave her a *Really, woman?* look.

"Oh, come on," she said. "I was kidding about the grandkids part; however, that doesn't mean that I don't want you to at least try."

I was about to argue back but she cut me off.

"Nuh-uh," she said with her hand up. "Just. Try."

I took a deep breath. "Yes, Ma." I made my voice as convincing as possible.

She squinted her eyes, probably thinking whether or not I was just saying that to appease her. "Good," she said, and she kissed my cheek before walking toward my front door. She paused before leaving. "Get out," she said.

"What?" I said.

"Get out. Go out. Whatever. Just be out of this house for a couple of hours. Go somewhere outside these four walls." She waved her hand. "You need a change of scenery."

I didn't respond because I knew she was right.

With one last smile, she closed the door behind her.

I was all alone in that house. I was scared and nervous and, most of all, I was tired.

I was tired of feeling like this and acting like a victim. My mind replaced my neurosis with anger.

I stood there for a couple of minutes thinking about our conversation. She was right on pretty much everything except the whole Sebastian thing. I didn't want to tell her that ship had sailed and we hadn't spoken since the texts on Sunday. I hadn't contacted him for my own reasons, and he'd obviously realized that I was a mess, so he'd made no effort to see how I was.

"Fuck it," I said out loud.

I grabbed my keys and locked the door behind me on the way to my car. I got in and pulled out of the driveway. My mind turned on autopilot and, the next thing I knew, I was parking in front of Thunders. I didn't know why I was there, but subconsciously it felt right.

I didn't want to meet anyone or cruise the place for a hookup. I just needed to be out among the people instead of locked in my house.

Alcohol being readily available wasn't a bad thing either.

Fuck. Do I talk about getting drunk a lot? I'm really not an alcoholic, but damn, I've mentioned wanting to get plastered a lot, haven't I?

I didn't bother to check my breath or see if I had any eye boogers before I got out of the car and walked over the threshold of the bar's entrance.

There was barely anyone there and none of them paid attention to me, which was perfectly fine with me. It was still kinda early for the Friday night rush, so it gave me a chance to plop down anywhere I wanted and not be bothered for a bit.

I ordered a Grey Goose dirty martini and downed it in one gulp, olives and all. It hit the spot I intended and made my face flush as my blood absorbed the alcohol.

"Another, please," I told the bartender, and he quickly made a second.

I sipped this one carefully and noticed that people had slowly started to file in. I felt like a creeper watching from a dark corner as the clientele strolled into the bar after a long workweek. Some were dressed to the nines while others looked like they'd just rolled out of bed.

Present company included.

By the time I finished my drink, the place was getting pretty busy. Some old, some young. Some drag queens and some guys who looked scared shitless. I tried not to think of Tyler.

I was feeling a little buzz and ordered another drink, since I had nowhere to go and another drink would pass the time. About halfway through my third drink and midway through the game of Candy Crush I was playing on my phone, I heard a familiar shriek that cut through the crowd and straight to my eardrums.

"*Guuurrrlsss!* I have arriiiiived!"

I looked up and saw Sean saunter in with his Fake and Bake entourage in tow. They reminded me of the plastic people from *Doctor Who*. I shrank in my chair and into the shadows so he wouldn't see me and swallowed the last of my martini so I could get the hell out of there. There will be no judging that finishing my drink took precedent over me running out of the place. I'd paid good money for that booze, thank you very much, and yes, I might have a problem. Shut up.

I stood too quickly and practically fell back onto the stool.

"Whoa." The bartender came over to me. "You all right, sir?"

"Uh… kinda?" I said, now a little dizzy mixed with drunk.

"Why don't I call you a cab?" he said.

"No, no," I said. "That won't be necessary. I will have someone pick me up. Thank you."

"You sure you're not going to leave here and hurt someone?" he asked.

"Promise. Look." I pulled out my phone and scrolled to Nicole's name. "I'm texting my sister right now."

And I did just that.

Nic, Drunk @ Thnders. Pick me up. U owe me.

She did, after all those times I'd had to pick her up from various bars when she was in her early twenties.

"See?" I said to the concerned-looking bartender. "All done."

He smiled, and I placed some money on the bar for my drinks and a healthy tip.

"Have a good night. I'm going to go wait outside."

I got off the barstool slowly and walked as quickly as I could with a stomach full of vodka. I kept my eye on Sean as I made my way to the exit and, of course, did not see the large man just standing there minding his own business, talking to his friends. I practically bounced off the man's chest and fell right on my ass in front of everyone, including Sean.

He looked down at me and began to laugh.

"My, my," he cackled. "If it isn't Daddy Warbucks." He looked around the bar. "Where is Little Whorephan Annie?"

I stood up and apologized to the gentleman I had run into before I turned and glared at Sean.

"I don't know who you're talking about," I lied.

He only laughed more. "I guess your bank account wasn't big enough for the LA gold-digging slut after all," Sean said in a tone I assumed was supposed to convey pity. The plastic people behind him snickered, and I longed for a sonic screwdriver.

"That's really none of your concern," I said quietly. I held on to the side of my pants tightly instead of putting my fist through his face.

"I did try to warn you," he said with a wag of his finger. "Well, I forgive you. Come give me a hug and we'll forget all about this whole fiasco. Friends again?"

He opened his arms wide, waiting for me to hug him.

I was toasted enough and wrapped in self-pity to the point that I almost did hug him.

Luckily, some rational voice screamed *Are you fucking nuts?* in my head.

I looked at him as he moved his arms up and down for acknowledgment. I started to laugh, and I mean laugh. He just stood there as everyone around us shifted their glances between me and him, confused.

My eyes were tearing up because I was laughing so hard.

He dropped his hands. "What is so fucking funny?"

"Oh, Sean," I said, finally controlling my giggle fit. "We were never friends."

"Excuse me?" he spat.

"Let me think about it… no, Sean, I won't. And you know why? Because there really is no excuse for you," I said. "You're an awful person with no soul." I paused for half a second. "You know what, that is being mean to soulless people like gingers and demons. You're worse than that, Sean. You know what you are? You're a fungus. A nasty, mold-like fungus that just grows on people, and no matter how hard we scrub, there you are again. I mean, we could wash and disinfect, but at the end of the day, if you have Sean in your life, you're going to have to just accept the fact that he is there to stay."

A few gay gasps spouted from behind him, and Sean's face went into a snarl, then a smile. "You're just jealous of me. You always have been. You always wanted me. Unfortunately for you, I have no interest in hairless trolls." He laughed, though only a few of his cronies joined him this time.

I tilted my head and walked closer to him. "I am jealous, Sean. You figured me out. Because Cher knows I have always wanted to be such a pathetic bitch that I have to drug people to get them to go home with me." More gasps. "Of course, you need to drug them because they're not aware that your online pic is so old it was probably taken with a Polaroid. So when they show up to meet you, you need that extra narcotic boost to make sure they don't go screaming into the night."

With each word I moved toward him.

"Running away from the—" Step. "—Fat—" Step. "—Old—" Step. "—Washed up—" Step. "—Fungus."

Everyone around him dropped back a foot, and his face turned white.

In a voice so low that only he and I could hear, I said, "Next time you want a battle of wits, let me check my brain at the door and we can start fair."

I blew him a kiss and turned toward the exit.

My body shook with adrenaline after I said to Sean what I'd been holding back for years.

I walked out of the bar with my head held high and threw up three steps later.

However, my stomach couldn't hold back the alcohol as it switched to the spin cycle.

Luckily it wasn't the chunky variety since I hadn't eaten anything all night. After one last heave, I opened my eyes to see a pair of familiar boots to the left of Vomit Bay.

"You've got to be shitting me," I whispered and rose slowly. I turned to see Sebastian staring at me with a look of concern mixed with pity.

"What the hell are you doing here?" I slurred but only slightly, I swear. With the adrenaline gone, the drunkenness came back in full force.

"I came to see if you were all right," he said in a monotone.

"Peachy fucking keen, jelly bean." I swayed in place.

He shook his head. "You look like shit."

"And you don't, so now we're even!" I yelled because that totally made sense to drunk me. "Leave me alone. My sister should be here any minute."

"No, she won't," he countered.

"Yes, she will. I just texted her."

"I know," he said. "She called me and told me to come get you."

I stopped pacing up and down the road. "That fucking bitch. I'm gonna kill her as soon as I can get a ride to her house!" I pulled out my phone and almost dialed Tyler to come pick me up from Texas.

"Rob," Sebastian said as he came toward me. "Come on."

"No! Get away from me!" I tried to walk around him, but he grabbed both my hands, and I tried in vain to escape his grasp. No such luck when he had about fifty pounds of muscle on me and I had a gallon of Grey Goose flowing through my veins.

"Sebastian, let me go!" I wiggled helplessly.

"No," he said sternly and reached up to touch my cheek with one hand.

"I can't do this," I pleaded and smacked away his hand. "I thought I was ready, but I'm not." I was losing a battle with my tear ducts.

"You barely even tried," he said.

"No!" I got up in his face. "Don't you talk to me like you know anything about me!"

"You're right. I don't," he said. "You're not giving me a chance."

"And you should be thanking me for that!" I yelled.

He didn't say a word.

"You wanna know a little more about Robert DeCaro?" I asked. He didn't indicate he wanted to, but I kept going. "Have you experienced a loss so great that you can't function for days on end and in turn have anxiety attacks so bad that you pass out because you think you're about to die?"

He stared at me, and I felt my body shake.

"I didn't think so." I pointed to my head. "You don't want to know what goes on in here every day."

He stood there speechless.

"Exactly," I said and turned away from him.

"My mother almost killed herself when I was nineteen," he said.

I whipped back around to face him. "What?"

Sebastian took a deep breath. "When I was a senior in high school, she got pregnant completely by accident. My parents weren't planning on having another child, considering their only child was about to graduate, but things happen and they were happy." He took another deep breath. "Unfortunately something went wrong just before the second trimester, and she had a miscarriage. At first, she accepted that it just wasn't meant to be, but my father and I knew that it affected her more than she showed. She acted normal up until I left for LA."

He scratched his head nervously as I stood there trying to stay upright. His words were starting to sober me up.

"There was a little piece of me that felt terrible for leaving, but my dad said everything was fine." He reached up and wiped a tear from his eye. "It was all 'fine' until the depression started. She would stay inside and not want to leave. She would go for days without speaking or even eating. When she finally did get her appetite back, she would eat very little and lost a lot of weight. It just made everything worse."

I started to walk toward him but stopped when he started to speak again.

"My father called me and told me that he needed my help. I took the first flight I could and met up with him at Kings Park Psychiatric Hospital." He scratched his head again. "The doctors said that they were able to pump out the pills she took and gave her an IV to replenish the lack of food intake. They kept her there for a week before we could bring her home. The doctors told us that even though they gave my mother some antidepressants, she was still prone to panic attacks since losing a child was so traumatic."

I moved a little closer.

"I stayed another week before I told my father I needed to get back," he continued and stopped walking. "I knew he wanted me to stay, but I just couldn't. He made up an excuse that he wanted to be alone with my mother anyway." He looked at me with hurt eyes. "I should've stayed, but I was too chickenshit to deal with it."

I stood there and didn't know whether to hug him or slap him across the face.

"Just because I don't know what you've been through, doesn't mean I don't know that it hurts," he said.

"But you left," I breathed.

"Yes." He sounded exhausted.

"What makes you think that you won't do it again?" I asked. "What if I lose it one day and you give up on me like you did with your mom?"

I regretted what I said as soon as it fell out of my mouth.

He looked like I'd driven a stake through his heart. "I won't," he mumbled.

"Bullshit," I said. "Let me save you the trouble. I'm out of here."

I turned and staggered down the side of the road to where my car was parked.

"Where the hell do you think you're going?" I heard Sebastian call from behind me. "Rob! You're fucking plastered. You can't drive anywhere!"

"Fine! Then I'll walk home!"

"You live on the other side of town!" he yelled. "Come on, man! Let me drive you!"

I whipped around a little too quickly and almost fell due to vodka dizziness. "*I don't need anything from—*"

My vocal chords went numb because I saw the dark shadow of Sebastian's frame surrounded by the bright headlights of a car speeding toward him.

"*Noooo!*" I screamed before the tunnel vision kicked in and my knees buckled under me.

My ears were ringing so I didn't hear but only felt the wind of the car zoom past me.

"Not again, not again, not again!" I repeated as I held my head in my hands and rocked back and forth on the gravelly ground. My palms were saturated with tears because, even if I could see, I didn't want to look up.

"Why…. Why…?" I asked the now muddy ground.

I don't know how long I sat there, but the next thing I knew, I was being lifted up by two hands on my shoulders.

I kept my eyes closed even though my head flopped around on my neck like a wet noodle.

"Rob," a voice said. "*Rob!*" the voice repeated more loudly as the hands on my upper arms shook me. "I'm here. C'mon, babe, open your eyes. You're fine. I'm here."

I felt one of the hands move to the side of my head and lift it up slowly. The thumb traced my eyebrow and down to my temple.

I pressed my face against the palm and slowly opened my eyes. They had been closed for so long that the light from the streetlamp above me stung my retinas.

"I'm here," Sebastian whispered, gently rubbing the side of my head.

"How?" My voice cracked.

"How what?" He slowly slid his palm around to the back of my neck and massaged it tenderly.

"The car. I thought...." I was attempting to stand while still trying to figure out how Sebastian survived the crash. "It happened again."

"What are you talking...?" He paused and looked behind him. "Oh...." He turned back at me.

I stared into his eyes, waiting for an answer.

"Rob," he spoke carefully, "that car was nowhere near me."

I shook my head in disbelief.

He put both of his large hands on either side of my face. "I'm okay." I shook my head again. "Yes, and so are you."

I tried to shake my head more, but his fingers wouldn't allow it.

"Why?" I asked.

He looked confused. "Why?" he repeated.

"Why are you here?" I clarified.

"Because," he responded.

"That's not an answer, Seb," I said.

"Well, ask a better question." He smiled slightly.

I glared at him, waiting for a real response.

"Because I was worried about you. Is that a better answer?"

"I don't know," I muttered quietly.

He dropped his shoulders and his left hand.

"What do you want me to tell you, Rob?" he asked, taking half a step away from me. "Do you want me to tell you that I've been going nuts thinking about the past week and not talking to you? Is that it? Do you want me to tell you that your sister got so sick of me asking about you that she finally relented and told me where you were going to be?"

I cried silently into the hand that was still attached to my face.

"Do you want me to tell you that even though this whole situation is fucking bizarro and I'm scared shitless, I still really, really like you?"

I stood there for a minute and looked at him blankly.

"Why?" I asked again.

"I don't know," he said. "Do I have to have a reason?"

I shrugged. "I have no fucking clue anymore, but I can give you a million and a half reasons why you shouldn't like me."

He crossed his arms. "Oh yeah? Try me."

"I'm a fucking mess, Seb," I said. "I'm terrified of not being in control of everything in my life, especially the fate of my relationships. I'm scared of you leaving me for someone better or me falling to my death or you getting run over by a phantom car because you were following me."

Sebastian looked like I had just run over his heart with a steamroller.

"By that look on your face, I can tell you're already getting freaked out, so it was nice knowing you." I turned and started to walk again, but he spun me around.

"Do you think I don't have any of those fears?" he said, his eyes full of pain. "While they may not be as specific as yours, it doesn't mean I'm not shitting bricks over here."

"I can't lose someone else, Seb," I said, "I don't want someone to leave my life again."

"And I'm going to try my best not to," he said, placing his hands on my shoulders and forcing me to look into his green-brown eyes. "If I have to lock myself in a padded room, covered up in bubble wrap head to toe, I will." He smiled warmly.

I shook my head but couldn't help but smile back.

He pulled me in for a hug.

"And what if something does happen?" I asked with my head against his chest.

He pulled me away to look into my face again. "Really, Rob? We're starting this again?" His face was more upset than angry.

"Some absurd situation that I concocted in my head could actually come true," I said. "I mean, there are guys prettier and saner than me not even twenty feet from where we stand. They can offer you so much more than I ever could. They have less crazy in their family trees and don't think about death every ten minutes." I paused for air. "Just saying."

He took a deep breath. "Are you done or would you like to take my voice away too, Ursula?" he said dryly.

I cocked an eyebrow and sniffed. "If I wasn't so flattered you called me that, I would hit you."

"Only if I let you," he said with a sinister smile.

I wiped my eyes, crossed my arms, and gave him a once-over. "Let us not forget that I know how that first date almost ended," and I nodded at his crotch.

His face scrunched up. "How could I forget?" He shielded his dick behind his hands.

I laughed, and he smiled back, still protecting himself.

I stepped closer to wrap my arms around him, and he slowly wrapped his around me. I rubbed up and down the outline of his spine lightly while he did the same with my hips.

"You really do like me, don't you?" I asked after a few minutes. I raised my chin and leaned against his chest, looking up at his scruffy jaw.

"Is this a trick question, because haven't I already established that I do in this conversation?" His face looked confused and impatient.

I let out a long breath. "I just want to make sure. Despite my irrational neurosis, my imminent baldness, and the fact that my mother lives fifty feet away from my front door, you're sure you still want to be with me."

"Pretty sure." He nodded slowly just to make sure I understood.

I rolled my eyes. "You must be really as fucking nuts as I am. You know that, right?"

He dropped his head back and squinted at the sky like he was searching for the answer. When he found it, he pulled his face close to mine. "Yes, you neurotic, balding bitch."

I smiled widely. "Good to know, you crazy, antler-wearing asshole."

He matched my smile, and I stood on my toes while he bent to kiss me.

I WOKE up slowly to the sound of two people talking on the other side of my bedroom door, which I didn't remember closing before Sebastian and I went to bed. I heard the bass that was no doubt Sebastian's voice and another that was familiar but not as deep.

I blindly searched my nightstand for my glasses and put them on. Once out of bed, I walked slowly to the door. The closer I came to the voices, the better my hearing got, and I recognized the other voice. I counted to ten silently and opened the door.

"Oh God, did he tell you the one time he got stuck in a tree because he said that princes only rescue princesses if they're really high in the air?" my uncle said to a now hysterically laughing Sebastian.

"No," Sebastian said through his tears, "he didn't. I don't think he'll be doing that anytime soon. Unless he gets that weave he always wanted."

Now both of them were practically on the floor laughing.

At my expense, no less.

"What the hell is going on out here?" I asked loudly, which surprised them both—and only calmed their laughing fit a tiny bit. I turned to my uncle. "And to what do I owe the displeasure?"

They both stopped laughing, and my uncle straightened and walked over to me.

"I came to apologize," he said, then looked over at Sebastian and back at me, "to both of you."

"Oh?" I said and crossed my arms.

"Yes," he said. "I didn't know if you were even home since your car wasn't in the driveway, but to my surprise, and delight if I must say, Sebastian was up going through your cabinets, no doubt looking for some dead animal to consume."

"Hey...," Sebastian protested.

"Really, Sven?" James cocked an eyebrow.

Sebastian looked at me and shrugged.

He was shirtless and cute, so I couldn't really be mad at him.

I looked back at James, still waiting for the rest of his story.

"By that nasty look on your face, I'm sure you want a list of what I'm sorry for, correct?" he asked.

I said nothing but nodded my head.

"Well, since I was a complete and utter twat to Sebastian the first time I met him, it seemed the universe was doing me a favor, in more ways than one, by having him answer your door half-naked and not throwing me into the pool," my uncle said.

I looked over to Sebastian. "Besides the slightly pedophilic talk, is this true?"

Sebastian nodded his head. "Yup."

I switched back to James. "Continue."

"Certainly, Your Honor." He curtseyed, and I rolled my eyes. "I told Sebastian, as I'm about to tell you, that I'm a professional bitter queen who loves his family so much that he may come off as an overprotective and unfiltered old coot." He moved closer to me and put his hand on my shoulder. "I only want the best for you, and sometimes I get so caught up in the past that I forget the future doesn't have to be a repeat."

I continued to stare at him.

"I made an assumption about Sebastian, and I was wrong. The older you get, the more convinced you are that there are only four different types of people in the world, and you don't like any of them. This one is obviously a character all unto himself, and I am not too proud to admit I was wrong."

"You most definitely are old," I said, "and quite possibly senile." He shrugged, and I uncrossed my arms to grab his shoulders. "But, you're *my* old, senile, and extremely bitter uncle who taught me everything I need to know about being a man in this fucked-up, far from Neverland world." I smiled at him. "And I love you for that."

I pulled him in for a hug.

"Aww, man," Sebastian said. "You're going to make me cry!" He got off the couch and wrapped his arms around both of us, squeezing tightly.

"Oh my God," James said through shallow breaths. "This is just all sorts of wrong on so many levels right now."

"I know," I strained. "Seb, honey, we're not that kind of a family. This isn't backwaters Mississippi."

He let us go, and we finally came up for air.

"Geez." Sebastian stood there with his hands on his hips. "Do you two ever not have your minds in the gutter?"

James and I looked at each other, then back to Sebastian. "No," we said in unison and started cackling like the Sanderson sisters.

Sebastian stood there with a pouty look on his face. "Fine. I'm going to go put a shirt on, then," he said as we whined jokingly. He turned his nose up in the air and walked into the bedroom, closing the door behind him.

"He's quite the doofus, isn't he?" James asked me.

"Yeah," I said. "He's a cute doofus too." I smiled.

"I like him," he said.

I looked at him. "But...."

"No 'but.' I like him and that's all."

"Okay, then," I said. "I like him a lot. I mean, I don't know where this is all going, but I'm excited and scared for the journey."

James gasped. "Why, Miss Elsa, does this mean that frozen heart of yours is finally melting?"

I shook my head. "Don't say it," I pleaded.

"Does this mean you 'let it go'?" He smiled and giggled like a two-year-old.

I sighed. "Why me?" I quietly questioned my lineage.

Sebastian, unfortunately with a shirt on, opened the bedroom door. "I heard the word 'but.' Were you guys just talking about my butt or just butts in general?"

I groaned.

"He's all yours," my uncle whispered in my ear, and I nodded. He paused when he reached my front door. "Oh, by the way…." He turned to face me. "Your mother is making breakfast for a small country, and she wanted me to tell you boys that you're more than welcome."

I looked over at Sebastian, staring at me like a puppy begging for a treat, drool and all.

"Tell her we'll be there in a bit," I said to my uncle, and Sebastian almost did a backflip.

"Oh, okay," James said. "A little something first to work up your appetite?" He winked at me.

"*Out, demon spawn!*" I yelled and slammed the door behind him.

Sebastian looked at me with a different hunger in his eyes.

"No," I said. "I don't do quickies."

"Oh, all right," he said, defeated.

"I like to take my time," I said seductively.

"Good," he said seriously, "'cause I'm not going anywhere."

I stopped dancing sexy and looked at him.

His face was like marble and didn't move. His eyes, however, looked so warm and sad at the same time.

I walked over to him and stood up on my tiptoes to look him straight in the eye.

"We'll just see about that," I whispered.

He smiled as he wrapped my legs around his waist. "Challenge. Accepted."

He grabbed the back of my neck and pulled me into a deep kiss.

I pulled away after a minute or five.

"Later," I panted. "I promise."
"Fuck, yeah," he said and put me down gently.
I smiled. I smiled at him and I smiled at myself.
I can do this, I thought. *I finally can do this.*

FROZEN HEART Status: Melted

Epilogue
A Way Back to Then

"SEBASTIAN!" I yelled out the window. "I told you not to put the comforter in the dryer without any dryer sheets! We might as well be sleeping in an electric chair!"

"Sorry!" he yelled back from shoveling the snowy driveway. "I love you!"

He grinned widely. Half his face was covered in an Eskimo-type hat and a thick scarf, even though he'd grown a little bit of a beard and mustache for the winter months.

He looked quite fetching, so I rarely stayed mad at him for long.

"Yeah, yeah!" I called back. "Love you too, but at this particular moment I don't know if I like you."

I closed the window and shivered from the cold.

"After six months, you think the man would've learned how I do laundry by now," I said out loud.

We hadn't "officially" moved in with each other, or should I say, he hadn't officially moved into my little cottage behind my mother's house yet, but he was there at least six out of seven days a week, since it was an easier commute from my house to his job than it was to drive from his parents' house in the next county.

He would go there every couple of days to get clothing or some other thing he "needed" from there, which made laundry fun and my house look like it was closing in on itself.

Oh, who am I kidding? We live together.

There, I said it. Are you happy now?

Yeah, I know what you're going to say. We're moving too fast or I'm nuts for letting someone live here rent-free or some other thing that's going to annoy me.

Let me just say, number one: Thank you for the concern. I appreciate the gesture. For serious.

And number two: No, I don't have a warped reality of love at first sight or some bullshit like that. I really do love Sebastian and for some stupid reason he loves me back. I mean, he's big and doofy and sexy as hell while I'm just... me.

But I guess that does it for him.

You're not supposed to know how love works, because if we did, there wouldn't be so many cat ladies in the world.

You're probably also wondering, how is the relationship compared to the one I had with Riley.

If you weren't thinking about that, I'm going to tell you anyway.

Riley was the prince on the white horse whom I needed to get me out of the life I was in years ago. While Foster wasn't a shiny castle, I didn't want anything else. We rarely argued and he gave me anything I wanted, whether material or not. There wasn't much I wanted, but I was happy to know the offer was always there.

Then he left me.

I had nothing.

The castle was empty and the glass slipper had shattered into a thousand pieces.

After some time, I tidied up the castle and fixed that damn shoe all by myself. Except I never put it back on, but instead locked it in the highest tower to prevent it from being broken ever again.

When I moved back here to the provincial town I grew up in, I didn't want anything to do with anyone except my family, and I certainly didn't want to find love.

Especially with the guy who looked like he should be delivering ice to the local royalty.

We bicker like we're eighty practically every day.

"Can you *please* change the toilet paper when there's one goddamn sheet left?"

"Fuckin' A! Why are you making me watch this show about werewolves in high school? And why hasn't that one with the eyebrows fucked that kid with ADHD yet?"

I'd bitch about him leaving his dirty underwear in the middle of the room, and he'd complain that I was starting to sound like my mother.

You know, "normal" couple things like that.

I can't explain it, but it just works.

Sebastian is exactly what I need.

He's a big teddy bear with a body like a guardian of the galaxy. He has never disrespected me and has never taken any of my bullshit either.

He never judges my little OCD moments, but he has helped me overcome some of them.

My family loves him—yes, even my at-first-judgmental Uncle James. James only wanted the best for me, but once he got to know Sebastian, James saw what he did for me. He hasn't told me directly, but from what my mother has hinted, Sebastian and I remind my uncle of him and Andy.

Okay, and maybe my uncle thinks Sebastian's cute too. I don't know.

Sebastian has never been jealous or uncomfortable if my sister or mother mention Riley during a conversation. He knows I had a life before him, and he knows what Riley meant to us all.

He has never made any attempt to make us think that he's better than Riley or that he's here to fill the holes in our hearts.

He's Sebastian and he's different. He isn't here to impress anyone and that's what makes him so impressive.

And yes, the sex is pretty amazing. I know your minds are there and that's why we get along so well.

As I tried not to get electrocuted while folding my Target comforter, my phone rang.

I hit Accept and answered. "Well, well. If it isn't the sporting goods queen himself. To what do I owe...." I heard crying on the other end of the phone and dropped the comforter onto the floor.

My face and mood plummeted. "Tyler, what's wrong? ... An accident? ... No, I haven't heard from him. ... Yes, I'll take the next flight I can. ... I'll let you know the details. ... Bye."

I hung up the phone and placed it on the kitchen table. I went into the living room and popped open my laptop, typing in Southwest Airline's website address to search flights from Long Island to Texas.

I was so involved in trying every airport combination I could think of and looking up car rentals that I didn't even hear Sebastian come in from outside.

"Holy shit, I feel great!" he bellowed, taking off his boots. The snow dropped on the carpet around him. "Fuck! I didn't mean to do that."

When I didn't complain about the rug getting wet, he put the boots down and walked over to where I was sitting.

"What's wrong?" he asked sternly.

I shook my head and kept looking for a better flight plan. Faster.

He sat down on the couch in front of me and waited there patiently. He knew that when I was in one of my "moods," he was safer to let me be for a few minutes before asking what was wrong again.

I finally found a flight that was leaving in the morning. About to type the number of tickets I wanted, I paused and looked across at Sebastian, who was playing with his scarf.

As much as I didn't want to listen to that bitch of a voice in the back of my head that kept asking me why Sebastian was with me, I figured this would be the perfect opportunity for the final exam.

"So," I said, and he looked back at me. "Ever been to Texas?"

Keep reading for
an exclusive excerpt from

When I Grow Up

A Tales from Foster High Story

By John Goode

After graduation, Kyle Stilleno and Brad Graymark move to California to pursue their dreams. But high school sweethearts are called that for a reason, and their love rarely stands up to the test of time. As money, school, sex, and jealousy test their relationship to the breaking point, Kyle and Brad fight to hold on to the love that brought them together.

But when a frantic phone call sends them back to Texas, they discover love and understanding might not be enough this time.

Coming Soon to
http://www.dreamspinnerpress.com

Kyle

YOU KNOW what, grown-ups? Fuck you. No, don't give me that look. I'm talking to you. Yes, you, the grown-up with the kids and the job and the bills, the person who pretends you know what is going on. Fuck you.

We spend our entire life thinking that when we get older, we're going to know what's going on and how to handle it. You give us this illusion that you know what you're doing, so of course in time we'll figure it out too. It's a generational lie, and I don't care if your parents did it to you 'cause I'm talking to you right now. And I know my mom wasn't mother of the year, but you know, she used the same damn line on me every time.

How dare you? How dare you lie to us like that and give us hope that someday the world will make sense! What possible reason do you have for perpetuating a lie as big as this one? I thought the whole Santa thing was mean; the Easter Bunny, not so much. It's a giant rabbit, please. But the thought of a magical fat guy sneaking into our house and leaving us stuff is more believable than what you tell us. Why not just say it out loud?

You have no idea what you're doing either.

Life sucks and, no matter how old a person is, it never makes sense. There's no instruction manual. Living on your own and paying your own bills isn't going to give you secret knowledge. If you had just admitted you were adult fuck-ups when people like me were kids, then we might be ready for all the crap when we graduated. We'd know there is no magical bullet for our ignorance, just more questions and a lot of improvising.

Do you get a power trip from making us believe you have answers when you don't? Is acting all-knowing a survival technique? If you'd told us you were clueless, did you believe we might panic and run around like we were on fire?

I think we could have figured it out together. If you'd told us "There are no answers, and we're all just making it up," I really think we kids would have said, "Let's make it up together."

But no, you go on how things will make sense when you're older and one day you'll understand. Well, here I am, waiting. And it makes no fucking sense. Instead I'm sitting in an airport typing so hard on my laptop I'm pretty sure they're going to call security on me. There are no answers at the bottom of that cereal box, just another useless piece of plastic designed to distract us from the abysmal pain that is life.

So tell me, grown-ups, tell me what I should do.

Leave him? Stay? Let her die in a hospital thousands of miles away? Tell me, give me a fucking answer.

Tell me which decision I make is going to be the right one.

Nothing? Not a single word? What a shock! Imagine my surprise! You don't know what to do any more than I do. I need to talk about this. I need to settle my thoughts in order and figure out the next best move I can make. My flight doesn't leave for two hours. So I'm going to figure this out on my own, since you don't have a freakin' clue.

I wanna say me sitting here alone started when he joined that idiotic softball league, but I know better; it started well before then.

When we moved into our new place, that first day, I should have said something, but I didn't.

And now here I am.

She is really going to die.

No, not there yet.

Eight months ago, Brad and I moved into our new place. And things started falling apart.

Don't miss how the story began!

Maybe With a Chance of Certainty

Tales From Foster High:
Book One

By John Goode

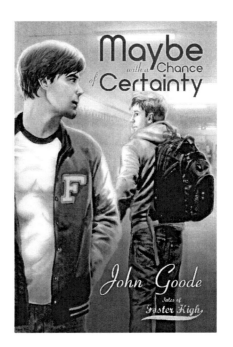

Kyle has worked hard at being the invisible student, toiling through high school in the middle of Nowhere, Texas. Brad is the baseball star at Foster High. Both boys are damaged in ways that the rest of the world can't see. When they bond over a night of history tutoring, Kyle thinks that maybe his life has taken a turn for the not-so-lonely.

He finds out quickly that the promise of fairy-tale love is a lie when you're gay and falling for one of the most popular boys in school, and if being different is a sin in high school, then being gay is the biggest sin of all. Now Kyle and Brad need to come to an understanding amidst the scrutiny of their peers or their fledgling relationship will crash and burn before it ever gets off the ground.

The End of the Beginning

Tales From Foster High: Book Two

By John Goode

Not too long ago, Brad Greymark outed himself to his high school and the rest of the town of Foster, Texas, with a fairly obvious public display of affection. Now what? Brad had thought being Foster's favorite son wasn't that important, but when it comes time to choose between high school fame and Kyle, the boy he might just be falling for? It's not an easy decision, knowing his heart may break either way.

http://www.dreamspinnerpress.com

Raise Your Glass

Tales From Foster High:
Book Three

By John Goode

Kyle Stilleno used to be the invisible student. Brad Graymark used to be the baseball star. Then they fell in love and Brad outed them both with a spectacular public display of affection, and now *everything* is different.

After spending a few days lying low, Kyle and Brad are going back to school. It's time to face the music and see how Foster High deals with their growing romance. But the school's reaction—and the staff's hostility—are not what they expected. Everyone they know seems to be allied against them. Isn't there anyone they can count on to defend their happiness?

http://www.dreamspinnerpress.com

Taking Chances

A Tales from Foster High Story

By John Goode

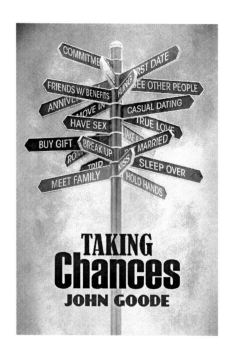

TAKING
Chances
JOHN GOODE

Fearing the backlash of living as a gay man in Foster, Texas, Matt Wallace runs away to California, only to find it isn't the Promised Land he'd hoped for. Christmas sees Matt returning to Foster, where he bumps into his old flame, high school jock Tyler Parker.

Now that they're older, it doesn't take Matt too long to figure out that love at first sight is a very real thing. The only problem is neither Matt nor Tyler seems to know what to do after that. They're both running from the past—and each other—requiring some reverse engineering to actually spur the relationship past the false start.

http://www.dreamspinnerpress.com

ROBERT HALLIWELL hails from the mysterious land of Ronkonkoma in the Island of Long and grew up dreaming of the day the dark, handsome Mediterranean Prince of his dreams would whisk him away from the boring life he was accustomed to to a land far, far away… from his mother. A magical place full of roller skates and rainbows called Xanadu. Unfortunately, that never happened, but he was instead whisked away to the dark kingdom of Westchester County and the "prince" turned out to be a very pale country bumpkin from Schenectady. Yes, it's a real place. When he's not spending the day writing, Robert can be found at home taking care of his four-legged children, Kira, Carter, and Willow, and viewing unhealthy amounts of QVC, much to the dismay of his husband, Kevin.

Robert is still waiting for Lynda Carter to sign the adoption papers he sent her in 1998.

Loving Jay

Renae Kaye

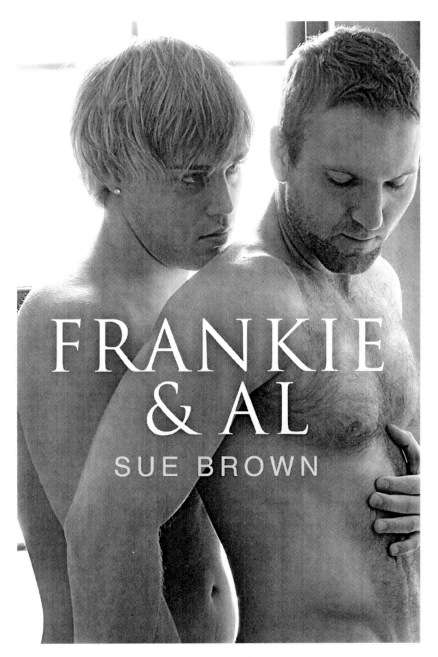

FRANKIE & AL

SUE BROWN

http://www.dreamspinnerpress.com

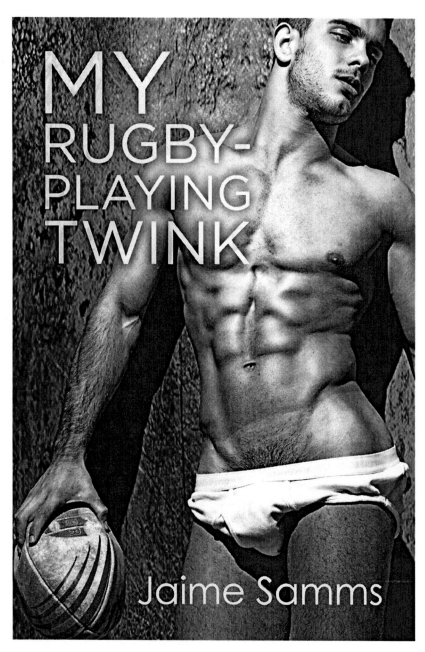

MY
RUGBY-
PLAYING
TWINK

Jaime Samms

http://www.dreamspinnerpress.com

Rat
Bastard

Stephen Osborne

http://www.dreamspinnerpress.com

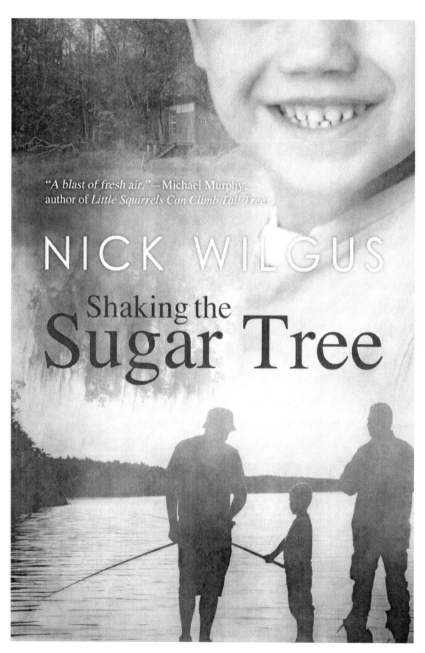

"A blast of fresh air." —Michael Murphy,
author of *Little Squirrels Can Climb Tall Trees*

NICK WILGUS

Shaking the
Sugar Tree

http://www.dreamspinnerpress.com

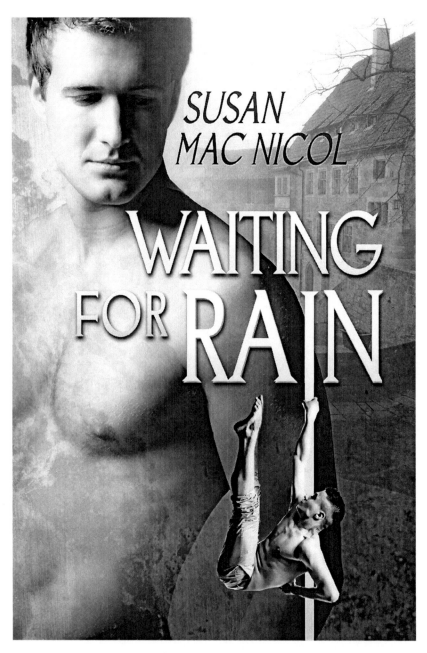

SUSAN
MAC NICOL

WAITING FOR RAIN

http://www.dreamspinnerpress.com

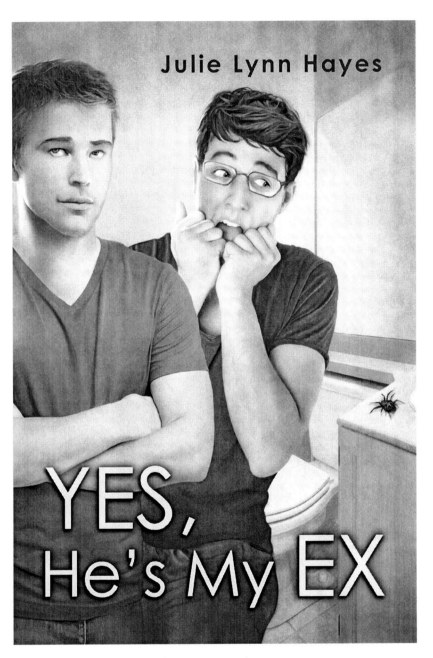

Julie Lynn Hayes

YES, He's My EX

http://www.dreamspinnerpress.com

Phoenix Emrys

The L Bomb

http://www.dreamspinnerpress.com

eli easton

the
Enlightenment
OF
DANIEL

http://www.dreamspinnerpress.com

CPSIA information can be obtained at www.ICGtesting.com
Printed in the USA
BVOW05s1228060815

411944BV00010B/154/P